JACO JACOBS

The Girl with WINGS

illustrated by
TORI STOWE

translated by
KOBUS GELDENHUYS

ROCK THE BOAT

A Rock the Boat Book

First published in Great Britain, the Republic of Ireland and Australia
by Rock the Boat, an imprint of Oneworld Publications Ltd, 2024

Published by arrangement with Pan Macmillan, South Africa. All rights reserved.

ISBN 978-0-86154-822-4
eISBN 978-0-86154-823-1

Printed and bound in Great Britain by Clays Ltd, Elcograf S.p.A.

Oneworld Publications Ltd
10 Bloomsbury Street
London WC1B 3SR
England

Stay up to date with the latest books,
special offers, and exclusive content from
Rock the Boat with our newsletter

Sign up on our website
rocktheboatbooks.com

MIX
Paper | Supporting
responsible forestry
FSC® C018072

CONTENTS

1

The boy at the window

"Wilson! Hey, Wilson, you still sleeping?"

Wilson gritted her teeth and pulled the duvet up over her head. It was far too early and too cold to even reply to such a spectacularly annoying question.

"Come on, Wilson!" called the muffled voice again, and she heard banging on the sliding window above her head. "I brought my dad's binoculars and a bird book. You promised you'd come with me."

"Urrrrghhh!"

With a groan,
Wilson sat up.
She opened the
curtains. A nose
was pressed flat
against the glass and alert
brown eyes sparkled excitedly when they saw her.

Wilson leant over and opened the window slightly.
She regretted this immediately. It felt as if she'd
opened a freezer door.

"I didn't *promise* to go with you, Errol," she said.
"I may have used words like *maybe* or *perhaps* or
I'll see what I feel like, but I definitely didn't *promise*."

Errol grinned. "Okay, see you in a sec. Bring something to eat. I like peanut-butter sandwiches with—"

Whap.

Wilson pushed the window shut without waiting
for the rest of his order. She wasn't about to make
sandwiches for some boy she hardly knew. Shivering
with cold, she climbed out of bed. She made sure the
curtains were closed before changing out of her
pyjamas and pulling on a pair of jeans, a long-sleeved
T-shirt and her warmest jumper.

Errol Abrahams was like a stray cat. A little more
than a week ago, he'd shown up uninvited, started
talking to her and promptly decided that they would
be friends. Never mind whether she liked him or not.

And she still hadn't decided that she did.

In the bathroom she quickly washed her face with ice-cold water from the tiny basin. The Doll's House was quiet. Her mum had already left to run her tennis camp, and Gabriel, her stepfather, was probably out somewhere taking photos again.

Wilson sighed, picked up her hairbrush and headed to the mirror. Trying to tame her long, light brown hair was her least favourite morning ritual. The curly bits around her ears always refused to join the pony tail party. One front tooth was a little crooked. That's why she avoided smiling in public. Someone who looked so ordinary shouldn't be living such a messy life.

If there was one thing Wilson Taylor had always longed for it was a normal life. On the inside of her wardrobe door she'd stuck an advert she'd torn from a magazine:

Why, you might ask? No, Wilson wasn't having trouble with a blocked nose. It was just because the people in the ad looked so *normal*. An ordinary dad, an ordinary mum and two ordinary children. The dad looked like someone who worked in an office and played golf on weekends. The mum looked as if she knew how to arrange flowers and cook a traditional South African roast with yellow rice and potatoes. The children… well, okay, she had to admit that the kids looked a bit irritating. The kind who never went to bed without taking a bath and cried when they didn't get full marks in a maths test.

But sometimes Wilson couldn't help wondering what it would be like to be part of such an ordinary family. The kind of family with a mum who hadn't named her daughter after a tennis racket. The kind of family with a dad who wasn't the Most Hated Photographer on Earth. The kind of family who lived in a proper house, with a garden, a pool and a dog; the kind of house that didn't have four wheels, and that couldn't move somewhere else overnight.

"Wilson!" called Errol impatiently from outside the Doll's House. Every time he called her name, he used a different voice.

A shrill, squeaky voice.

A croaky old man's voice.

A metallic robot voice.

"Wil—"

She yanked open the door of the Doll's House. "Okay, *okay*! I'm coming!"

Errol grinned broadly.

Wilson turned around and dashed to the food cupboard, quickly grabbing two oranges, a packet of biscuits and two cartons of apple juice. As she slipped them into her backpack, she spotted a curious Errol peeping in at the door of the Doll's House. He'd never been inside, and she wasn't planning to invite him in either.

Gabriel called the Doll's House a *motorhome*. A very fancy name for a very small house on wheels. It was basically like a caravan with its own engine. Gabriel bought it with the redundancy payout he received after he lost his job at the newspaper.

"Rosy-throated longclaw," said Errol, "Red-eyed bulbul, Black-headed oriole."

Wilson rolled her eyes as she stepped outside and locked the door of the Doll's House. "Are you okay? Do you have a fever or something? What's with all the strange talk?"

Errol pointed at the book in his hand. "Bird names," he said. "Pretty, hey? They sound like you could almost sing them."

Wilson replied with a snort. She could only hope that she wouldn't have to listen to him singing bird names on an empty stomach.

"Okay," she said and pointed at the binoculars in Errol's hand. "Where do you want to go to look for birds?"

"There are lots of trees next to the lake," said Errol. "And the more trees, the more birds."

Wilson planted her hands on her hips and stared at him, tilting her head to one side. "The lake on the edge of town?"

Errol nodded and started walking.

Wilson sighed and followed him.

When they'd lived in the city, her mum wouldn't allow her to go off on a Saturday morning with a boy who was a total stranger. But things were different in a small town. Everyone knew each other, and in the evenings the children played in the streets till dusk.

Wilson had stopped counting the number of towns they'd lived in over the past couple of years. Every time they would stay only a few months. Her mum would advertise her tennis camps for children, and the town's mums and dads would be impressed to have someone famous teaching tennis. While her mum taught children who barely knew how to hold a racket, Gabriel would explore the town and take thousands of photos. And when the children in the town had had enough of tennis lessons and Gabriel could find nothing else to photograph, they would pack up and hit the road in the Doll's House.

It had been almost three weeks since they'd arrived in Leseeba – and here she was now walking down a dusty road with a boy she hardly knew. She snuck a peek at Errol out the corner of her eye. He was whistling a familiar tune. Errol was her age, but a little shorter than her, and his arms and legs were as thin as matchsticks.

"Why birds, of all things?" Wilson finally asked.

The morning sun was warming the back of her neck nicely.

Errol shrugged. "Why not? My grandma says I have a different hobby every week. I found the book in the library and decided to see how many of the birds I can spot."

"There's one," said Wilson.

Errol looked up at the telephone wire she was pointing at. He smiled. "Sparrow," he said. "Okay, I'll tick it off."

"Did you know in the Sesotho language, leseeba is the word for feather?" Errol asked.

"Of course," Wilson lied.

"And where are the two of you going?"

The stern voice made Wilson jump. A policeman stopped his bicycle next to them. He had a grey moustache that was trimmed so perfectly that it looked as if it had been painted on his upper lip. His trouser legs were clipped with clothes pegs, probably to protect them from the oily bike chain.

"Captain Calitz," said Errol. "Good morning."

"Erm… morning," said Wilson.

The policeman sniffed. His perfect moustache twitched slightly on his upper lip.

"You haven't answered my question, Errol Abrahams," he said.

He looked so intimidating that Wilson swallowed nervously, but Errol was smiling. "Wilson and I are going to look for birds," he said.

Captain Calitz looked Wilson up and down and then he looked back at Errol.

"And where did you get that bird book and those

binoculars?" he asked.

"The book is from the library and the binoculars belong to my grandma," said Errol.

The policeman's eyes narrowed suspiciously. "Hmph," he said. His eyes shifted to Wilson again. "So, you're the girl who lives with her parents in that house on wheels in the caravan park?"

"It's called a motorhome," said Wilson.

"Hmph," said Captain Calitz again.

"Enjoy your day, Captain!" said Errol and started walking away.

Wilson had to hurry to catch up with him. She glanced over her shoulder. The policeman was still sitting on his bike like a statue, glaring at them. "Hmph," Wilson heard him snort again.

"What's his problem?" she whispered.

"Probably beetles again," replied Errol. "Or aphids."

Wilson waited for him to explain.

"He grows roses," said Errol. "All kinds and colours. His roses win lots of prizes at the annual flower show in the city. My mum says Captain Calitz's roses are like his children."

Wilson frowned. Small towns were weird. And clearly Leseeba was no exception.

"But why does he want to know where you got the book and the binoculars?"

Errol giggled. "Captain Calitz is a good policeman. He probably thinks I stole the book."

"*Stole* it?" Shocked, Wilson stopped in her tracks.

Errol nodded. "Yep. If you want to get technical. The thing is, I lost a library book once, more than a year ago. Now I'm no longer allowed to borrow their books. Miss Hannah, the librarian, is very strict. So I have to smuggle a book out of the library if I like it."

"*Steal* it, you mean," Wilson quickly reminded him.

"I always smuggle it back in afterwards," said Errol.

Wilson thought about that for a moment. "Well, a library is a place where you can borrow books and then return them. So, you're just borrowing books without a library card… sort of."

"Exactly," said Errol. "Rock pigeon."

He pointed at a bird and ticked off a name on the list at the back of the book. Wilson wanted to remind him that you weren't supposed to write in a library book, but then thought better of it. She'd known him for barely two weeks but that was long enough to know that Errol always had a clever comeback.

2

A feather

"Lesser masked weaver," whispered Errol.

Wilson frowned as she studied the picture in the book and shook her head. "Southern masked weaver," she said.

Errol lifted the binoculars again. "No way," he argued.

"Yes way," said Wilson and pointed at the book. "Look on the map. The lesser masked weaver isn't found in this area."

Before they could argue any further, the weaver flew off, chirping happily.

"Maybe that was a lesser masked weaver that got a little lost," said Errol.

Wilson rolled her eyes. She was starting to suspect that Errol wasn't as good at birdwatching as he thought.

They'd been at the lake for an hour now, looking for birds. Almost every new species they saw led to an

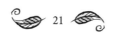

argument. Wilson had never known there were so many different types of birds that looked almost identical.

There was a grumbling sound.

"Your tummy's going to chase all the birds away," said Wilson. "Do you want an orange?"

"I thought you'd never ask," said Errol.

Wilson slipped her backpack off her shoulders and fished out the snacks she'd packed. They sat down on a patch of grass by the lake. The morning sun was shining brightly on the water. Two ducks swam by peacefully. (Cape shovellers, according to Errol, even though Wilson could clearly see that they looked exactly like the picture of the southern pochard in the book.)

Birds were warbling in the trees but by now Errol was more interested in peeling his orange.

"You never told me your mum was a famous tennis player," he said.

Wilson pressed the sharp end of the straw into the the carton of juice and took a sip before answering. "I haven't even known you for two weeks," she said. "So, I can't possibly have told you about me yet."

"I saw the ad in the café window," said Errol.

Wilson gritted her teeth. Every time they moved to a new town, her mum would cover it with her posters the minute they arrived.

All those capital letters and exclamation marks were enough to give anyone a headache.

"Did your mum really play tennis at Wimbledon?" asked Errol.

"Yes, of course!" said Wilson a little indignant. "Did you really think she would lie about something like that? Just Google her if you don't believe me."

"Don't worry, I believe you," said Errol. "And what about your dad?"

"Stepdad," said Wilson.

"I see him all over town with his camera. What kind of photos does he take?"

"He sells photos to an image library," said Wilson. "If someone needs a photo of a horse or a lemon or a stop sign, they can buy it from an image library."

"That's cool," said Errol and popped another segment of orange in his mouth.

"I don't think it is," said Wilson, rolling her eyes. "His top seller is a photo of a dog wearing sunglasses and a bow tie."

His second-bestselling photo was of a strawberry on a white background. Wilson would have to roll her eyes for an entire day to show what she thought of *that*.

Errol laughed. "And school?" he asked. "Don't you go—"

"Wow, you're asking more questions than Captain Calitz!" Wilson interrupted him. "Do you want to watch birds or pry into my entire family history?"

Errol shrugged. "I live with my grandma," he said, as if Wilson had asked. "She repairs people's clothes, does alterations and makes dresses for the school leaver's ball, stuff like that."

Wilson flattened her empty juice carton and put it into her backpack. She got up to wash the sticky juice off her hands in the lake.

As she was knelt by the water, she heard a rustling

sound in the trees. Wilson wheeled around and pricked up her ears. There wasn't a breath of wind. The leaves weren't moving at all.

Sometimes you get the feeling that someone is watching you… a strange, creepy feeling that makes the hair stand up on the back of your neck. Well, that was exactly how Wilson was feeling. She scanned the dense shrubs and trees next to the lake.

"Who's there?" she called.

"Shhh!" hissed Errol.

He must have heard the rustling too. He cautiously got to his feet and started creeping stealthily towards the trees.

"Come back!" whispered Wilson.

For all she knew, there were dangerous animals living close to the dam… leopards or crocodiles maybe. Or hippos. She'd once read that hippos were the most dangerous animals in Africa. Errol Abrahams might be a pain in the whatchamacallit but if a hippo were to gobble him up, she'd prefer not to be a spectator. He was so small that a hippo could swallow him trainers and all and still have space for dessert.

But, of course, Errol ignored her. He headed straight for the bushes. Wilson was still trying to decide whether it would be a good idea to follow him when she spotted something out of the corner of her eye. Only the slightest movement – a little leaf stirring.

She looked up…

   … and froze.

On a branch, quite high above her head, something was sitting.

No, not some*thing*. Some*one*. A girl. Her skin was the colour of golden syrup, and her dark hair hung loose over her shoulders. She was watching Wilson with large, startled eyes.

For a fraction of a second, it felt as if time had stopped.

Wilson could hear her heart thumping in her ears.

Then there was a fluttering sound.

When Wilson blinked, the girl was gone.

The branch was empty, as if she'd never been there.

Slowly, an object floated down to the ground. A leaf, Wilson thought at first.

But when she went closer and bent to pick it up, she saw what it was.

A feather.

Errol appeared next to her. He was breathless with excitement. "Was that her?" he asked. "Was that the bird girl?"

3

How was your day, Wilson?

"Somewhere, I'm still going to discover the next big tennis star," said Wilson's mum that evening when they were sitting outside under the extendable canopy. "But it won't be here in Leseeba. I'm not sure what the local kids do with their rackets but they definitely don't play tennis with them. Believe it or not, a child gave herself a mild concussion today when she tried to serve. Concussion! With her own racket! And the mum actually blamed *me*!"

"Oh," said Wilson. "Phew."

She was only half-listening to her mum's stories about that morning's tennis camp. She was lost in thought, staring at the beautiful grey-brown feather that she kept rolling between her fingertips. There were black stripes on the feather, with fine white specks in between.

"I took some lovely shots of an enormous pumpkin in someone's garden," said Gabriel, changing the subject.

"Maybe someone will buy them? I've never tried to sell shots of pumpkins."

Wilson didn't bother to respond to Gabriel. He was standing a little way off, stir-frying vegetables on the barbecue. It was freezing cold. He was wearing a thick jacket, a scarf and a beanie, and the tip of his nose was red. This wasn't exactly the right weather for preparing food outdoors but if Gabriel were to use the tiny kitchen in the Doll's House, the whole place would reek of fried green beans, carrots and mushrooms.

"So how was your day, Wilson?" asked her mum.

"Fantastic. I went birdwatching with Errol, the guy who lives opposite the caravan park, and we saw a girl with wings. She was sitting in a tree, right above my head. Look, here's a feather she dropped."

Of course, that wasn't at all what Wilson said. What she said was, "Oh, okay. Errol brought his bird book and binoculars, and we went birdwatching."

"You spot any unusual birds?" asked Gabriel.

Wilson hated it when he tried to sound interested in what she'd been up to.

"No."

Her mum shot her a warning look.

Wilson sighed. "We saw a kingfisher catch a frog. A malachite kingfisher. Errol thought it was a blue kingfisher."

"Really?" asked Gabriel. "Now, that isn't something you see every day. I wish I'd been there to take some photos."

Wilson grinned. If only Gabriel knew what *else* she and Errol had seen…

Errol had become all secretive when she'd asked him about the bird girl. "I'll tell you tomorrow," he'd said. "We *have* to come back tomorrow. And we have to be here first, waiting for her…"

He wouldn't say more than that, and then he rushed home for lunch.

Wilson was dying to know what he was going to tell her the next day.

4

Morning mist

The following morning, Wilson awoke at the crack of dawn when it was still dark outside and the Doll's House was quiet. Her mum and Gabriel were still asleep.

Wilson dressed quickly and tiptoed to the kitchen. She silently took out a loaf of bread, some peanut butter and apricot jam. She made herself and Errol a mountain of sandwiches, and put them in her backpack.

Outside, the first birds were starting to chirp in the trees and twitter in the morning cold.

Last night, Wilson had a dream about the bird girl, who was living in a large nest high up in the branches. Wilson had taken her some fruit and bird seeds. But the bird girl wasn't interested in any of it – she ate only wriggling pink worms.

Wilson tore a page from the pad on the fridge and quickly wrote her mum a message.

Errol and I
are going bird
watching X

She stuck it on the fridge door and quietly slipped out with her backpack on her back. The air was so cold that her breath made clouds. There was no sign of Errol. Maybe he was still sleeping. The grass in the caravan park was white with frost and it crackled like glass splinters under the soles of her shoes. They'd been living there for three weeks and no one else had showed up at the caravan park.

Wilson looked up. A white heron glided over her head, its wings flapping lazily.

The same questions that had kept her tossing and turning the night before like video games before bed were once again milling around in her head.

What was the secret of the bird girl? Was she just someone playing a prank? A girl wearing a weird feather coat? And how did Errol know about her – had he seen her before?

The moment she thought of Errol, she spotted him. There was a canary-yellow van parked on the other side of the street, close to his grandma's house. Errol was standing next to it, talking to the driver. A moment later the van roared off. Errol turned around and waved excitedly when he saw Wilson. He hurried over.

"Hey, Wilson!" he called.

"Who was that?" she asked.

Errol shrugged. "Just someone who wanted to know where the showgrounds are. Look, I brought you something."

He took a sheet of paper out of his hoodie pocket and held it out to Wilson. She unfolded it. It was an article cut out from a newspaper.

RUMOURS ABOUT "BIRD GIRL" UTTER RUBBISH

"Rumours that have been going around recently about sightings of a mysterious 'bird girl' are utter rubbish." That was the response of Captain Chester Calitz, head of police in Leseeba.

"There have been similar stories before. People really shouldn't take notice of them. Next thing, we'll probably hear there's a mermaid living in the town's lake!"

A local resident, Ms Janet Henderson, said that she regularly goes for a walk in the area. "Last Wednesday, when I was walking under the trees just outside town, I heard a rustling in the shrubs. She disappeared in a flash, but I saw her with my very own eyes – a child with wings. My first thought was that it was an angel, but she didn't have a halo and white wings like in all the angel pictures ... and I have to say, her face was really dirty."

According to Captain Calitz, there are several large bird species in this area, and he suspects that Ms Henderson saw either some species of eagle or bustard.

"What on earth is a bustard?" asked Wilson after she'd read the article.

Errol flipped through the bird book and handed it to her.

Kori Bustard: The kori bustard is the largest flying bird in Africa. An adult male kori bustard can reach a length of up to 1.35 metres and weigh between 15 and 40 kgs. They are usually found on open plains and, due to their size, they spend most of their time on the ground.

Kori Bustard □

"That wasn't what I saw," said Wilson.

Errol nodded. "I didn't think so."

Wilson bit her lower lip. "You weren't really planning to go birdwatching yesterday, were you?" she said. "You went looking for *her*."

Errol shrugged. "Maybe."

Wilson adjusted the straps of her backpack. "Well, then," she said, "what are we waiting for?"

The streets in town were Sunday-morning quiet.

On their way to the lake Errol didn't stop talking for one minute. He told her that his mum and dad worked in the city, that he only saw them once or twice a year, that his Granny Betty needed new glasses, about a TV programme on robots he'd watched and a book about germs he'd "borrowed" from the library. Wilson couldn't help smiling as she listened to him. Errol Abrahams' head was a very busy place indeed.

The lake looked like a mirror in the morning sun. It was so cold that fog was rising from the water. On the other side of the lake a thick layer of mist was hanging over the trees. The scene reminded Wilson of a fairy tale. She wouldn't be at all surprised if a unicorn or a dragon or a band of singing dwarfs appeared from among the trees. Or a girl with wings…

"Okay, so what's your plan?" asked Wilson.

Errol shot her a surprised look. "What do you mean?"

"How are we going to find the bird girl?"

Errol shrugged. "Maybe we should do exactly what we did yesterday." He raised the binoculars to his eyes. "Just sit here and keep our eyes on the trees."

It didn't sound like a brilliant plan to Wilson, but she didn't have a better one.

She and Errol sat on the same patch of grass where they'd eaten their oranges the day before.

"So, what does it feel like to live in a house on wheels?" asked Errol.

"It's small," Wilson replied, "and very chaotic. At least Gabriel built me my own little room with a door."

"How long are you going to stay here in Leseeba?"

"I don't know. Until my mum and Gabriel decide it's time to go."

"Is there a toilet in your—"

"Errol!" Wilson groaned. "Stop asking so many questions! It feels like a TV interview. Here, let's have a sandwich." She took the packet of sandwiches from her backpack and offered one to him.

"Peanut butter and apricot jam!" He smiled broadly. "My favourite!" Errol grabbed a sandwich and took a big bite. Fortunately, that kept his mouth occupied for a while. Wilson also took a sandwich, even though she didn't really like peanut butter.

Plop!

A fish leapt out of the water, making ripples on the surface of the lake.

Wilson put the half-eaten sandwich back in the packet. "Yes," she said.

Errol gave her a puzzled look.

"Yes, we do have a toilet in the Doll's House," she said.

They both burst out laughing. Wilson wasn't even sure why that was so funny, but she couldn't stop giggling. She snorted with laughter, and the sound surprised them both, making them laugh even louder.

"Ee-ee-ee!"

Wilson stopped laughing when she heard a strange sound. She pricked up her ears. Errol was still rolling on the grass with laughter. Wilson gave him a hard shove.

"Stop that, peabrain!" she hissed. "I heard something. Sounded like someone laughing."

"But that's what you and I were do—"

Wilson silenced him with a glare.

Plop!

Another fish leapt out of the water.

Wilson scanned the trees above them. The weird sensation that someone was watching them was crawling up her neck again...

"I think she's watching us," she whispered.

Errol jumped up. "Bird girl!" he called. "Where are you? Come out!"

A startled rock pigeon flapped away and disappeared deeper into the trees. Then everything was quiet again.

"Brilliant, Errol," said Wilson. "*If* she was here, you've just made very sure that we won't see her again."

"Hey, what did I do?" Errol asked.

Wilson didn't even bother to roll her eyes. She stood up and closed her backpack. "Captain Calitz was right – there's no bird girl. It was my imagination. We're wasting our time. I'm going home."

"You mean to the *Doll's House*," said Errol.

Wilson gritted her teeth and slung her backpack over her shoulder.

"Well, I'm going nowhere," said Errol. "I'm going to wait here until I see her."

"Good luck with *that*."

Wilson started walking off.

"Aren't you going to leave the sandwiches here?" Errol called after her.

His question fell on deaf ears.

Fortunately, the caravan park wasn't far away but the mist hanging over the trees made everything look spooky. Wilson walked a little faster and tried her best not to think of Little Red Riding Hood. She wished she hadn't agreed to come here with Errol – she could still be snuggled up in her bed. Maybe Gabriel would make breakfast outside on the barbecue, and then her mum would surprise her with breakfast in bed, instead of the horrible peanut-butter sandwiches she'd brought with her.

Plop!

Something struck her backpack with a muffled thud.

"Errol, you aren't funny!"

She kept on walking without looking over her shoulder.

Plop!

Something else hit her backpack and brushed past her shoulder. An acorn.

"Keep doing that, Errol. It isn't as if you're being childish or anything."

Plop!

Okay, now she'd had it. She wheeled around and…

…there was no sign of Errol.

"Errol?"

Her voice echoed through the trees in a weird, hollow way.

Ee-ee-ee!

Wilson felt her skin prickle with goosebumps.

"Who's there?"

There was a stirring among the bushes, only a few steps from where she was standing.

"Hello?"

She caught a glimpse of a green jumper among the leaves, and dark hair. Then the figure vanished again, and Wilson could hear rustling sounds further away among the trees.

"No, wait!" called Wilson in a shaky voice. "Come back! My name is Wilson. I... erm... I have sandwiches!"

It felt as if everything was holding its breath, even the trees and the bushes.

A face appeared from behind a thick tree trunk. Large brown eyes were watching Wilson suspiciously.

"There's no need to hide," said Wilson. "I won't bite."

The girl stepped out from behind the tree.

Wilson slowly breathed out. She was just an ordinary girl. She wasn't sure whether to feel relieved or disappointed.

"Hey," said Wilson. "What's your name?"

"Ava," said the girl. It sounded as if there were bells in her voice.

Wilson shrugged off her backpack and unzipped it.

"I still have loads of sandwiches," she said. "Would you like one?"

If she could believe her dream of last night, earthworms would probably have been a better idea. But, unfortunately, she didn't have any earthworms in her backpack.

The girl nodded.

Wilson opened her Tupperware of sandwiches and held them out to Ava. She reached out her hand to take one… then quickly pulled it back. But not fast enough. Wilson had already seen them. From under the sleeve of her jumper grey-brown feathers were sticking out.

5

Peanut butter and apricot jam

"You... you have feathers."

Probably not the smartest thing to say, but those were the first words to slip out of Wilson's mouth.

"Sorry, I mean... you obviously know you have feathers. All I meant was... you know... I don't mind, okay? Feathers are fabulous... I..."

Okay, that wasn't much better either.

"I've never met someone with feathers."

A faint smile formed at the corners of Ava's mouth. She reached out her hand again, and this time she took a sandwich.

Wilson tried hard not to stare at the feathers on the girl's hand.

Ava took a bite. "Peanut butter and apricot jam," she said.

Wilson nodded and pulled a face. "Sorry, it isn't my favourite either. It always makes me feel as if there's hair growing on my tongue."

Ava burst out laughing. The same bell-like laughter that Wilson had heard before. *Ee-ee-ee!*

Wilson grinned and also took a sandwich.

"Hair on your tongue," said Ava. "That's almost as weird as feathers."

Wilson wasn't quite sure what to say.

"No one must know that I'm here," whispered Ava. There was a strangeness to her voice – pleading, but also a little sad.

"Of course," said Wilson. "It's our secret."

She wasn't sure this was the right time to mention the newspaper story.

"It's her! You found her! Whoopee! I *knew* she really existed!"

Wilson let out a groan. Errol came charging towards them.

Ava dropped her sandwich and leapt back in fright, but Wilson held her hand.

"Don't worry, Ava," she coaxed. "It's only Errol. It's okay – you can trust him."

Ava's eyes darted anxiously in the direction of the trees. She looked down at Wilson's hand, which was still holding hers. For the first time Wilson felt the fine feathers under her fingertips. Immediately, she let go of Ava's hand – not because she was spooked by the feathers but because she didn't want Ava to think that she was trying to force her to stay.

"How did you find her, Wilson? Can she speak? What's her—"

"Shut up, Errol," hissed Wilson.

Errol's mouth snapped shut.

He was gawking at the fine feathers sticking out from under the sleeves of Ava's green jumper. You could almost see the questions bubbling up in his mind. Wilson noticed how Ava self-consciously pulled down her jumper sleeves. She suddenly felt very sorry for her.

"Tell you what," she said, "instead of us asking you a whole lot of questions, why don't you ask us something? Anything."

Errol and Ava looked almost equally surprised at this suggestion.

"Okay," said Ava. "How old are the two of you?"

"Twelve," said Wilson and Errol simultaneously.

"I'm small for my age," added Errol.

Ava bit her lower lip. "What are you doing here? I saw you yesterday as well."

Wilson and Errol exchanged an uncertain look.

"We came looking for birds," said Errol, and pointed at his binoculars and bird book as proof.

"But we actually came looking for you," Wilson

admitted. "Someone else saw you… It was in the newspaper."

Ava sighed. "I know," she said. "Believe me, my mums weren't very happy about that."

"Your mums?" asked Errol.

Wilson glared at him with a frown.

"Sorry," he said. "I forgot that it's your turn to ask questions."

Ava smiled. "Okay," she said, "last question. Can you guys keep a secret?"

"What secret?" asked Errol.

Wilson gave him one of her best eye-rolls. "Errol!" she said. "At least *try* to use the few brain cells you have."

"Oh!" It looked as if a light had been switched on in Errol's eyes. "You mean… a *secret*." He pointed at Ava.

The two girls grinned at each other.

"Okay," said Ava. "Now it's your turn."

Errol looked as excited as a dog that had heard the postman at the door. "You mean…?"

Ava nodded.

"Where do you live?" Errol fired away. "And who are your mums?"

"My mums' names are Ma Rita and Ma Zelna." She giggled, looking embarrassed. "Erm… I mean Rita and Zelna."

"The bee farmers!" Errol exclaimed excitedly.

Ava nodded again. "Our little farm isn't far from

here. But it can get quite lonely out there. I know every tree and every anthill like the back of my hand. So sometimes I come and… explore a little."

The next question burst out of Errol's mouth. "Why do you have feathers?"

"Errol!" scolded Wilson but Ava smiled.

"It's okay," she said, chuckling. "Why do some people have ears that stick out?"

Errol touched his ears self-consciously. "That's the way I was born," he said. "You can't do anything about it."

Ava shrugged. "Exactly."

"But this is different – I've never heard of someone who was born with *feathers*," said Errol.

Ava smiled mysteriously. "I'm sure there are *many* things you've never heard of…"

Wilson's eyes strayed to Ava's back. There was a strange bump, as if she was carrying a backpack under her jumper. Errol probably hadn't noticed it yet, or he would have said something. Wilson was dying to ask the question but it was stuck to her tongue like peanut butter, so she didn't.

She wanted Ava to share her secret of her own free will, and only when she was ready to do so.

6

Bean soup

"You won't believe what I saw today," said Gabriel that evening while they were eating.

Wilson felt like saying, *You won't believe what I saw today*. But instead she swallowed her words along with a spoonful of Gabriel's thick bean soup.

"There's a funfair in town," he said. "At the show-grounds. When I walked past there today, there was quite a commotion. People bustling about, setting up all the rides and things. There are posters all over town as well. I took some lovely shots of the big wheel."

"Can you believe it?" said Wilson's mum. "I never thought a funfair would come to a small town like Leseeba."

"Well, no one thought a former Wimbledon star would come to a small town like Leseeba to coach tennis," said Gabriel and winked at her mum. "But miracles do happen."

"Has anyone told you that you're adorable?" cooed Wilson's mum.

"Not as adorable as you," said Gabriel. "And beautiful too."

Had the soup not been so yummy, Wilson would have lost her appetite instantly. Gabriel was a pain, but she had to admit that his cooking was better than her mum's. Wilson's mum had even managed to burn two-minute noodles, reducing them to ashes. Unsure about how long you had to microwave them, she had zapped them for half an hour. Gabriel was a vegetarian and, in the beginning, it had been a little weird never to eat meat, but lately Wilson hadn't even missed it. Gabriel could make hundreds of fantastic dishes from memory – even though he had to cook most of them outside on the barbecue.

"You and Errol are spending a lot of time together these days," said Wilson's mum. "I'm glad you've made a friend."

Wilson just shrugged. "He's okay," she said.

Truth be told, she'd made up her mind long ago not to make friends with anyone any more. Because as soon as she made friends, they would inevitably move away. Friends were part of a normal life – the kind of life the family in the advert behind her wardrobe door had. It was too much trouble making friends when you knew you were going to lose them again after a few weeks.

Wilson immediately felt guilty about feeling sorry for herself.

She couldn't help thinking of Ava.

Ava's life was even *less* normal than hers. She was born with a secret – a secret that she would have to hide under that green jumper for the rest of her life, or else…

Wilson bit her lower lip absent-mindedly.

What would happen if people were to find out about Ava?

Her photo would probably be in newspapers all over the world. TV stations would queue up to interview her. Scientists might even decide to study her.

Wilson couldn't wait for the following day. She and Errol had agreed to meet Ava at the lake again. Wilson was desperate to find out more about her. About that hump under her jumper, of course, yes. But more than that – she wanted to know what it felt like to have such a different life. A life that was even more different than her own.

"Gosh, Gabriel," said her mum with a giggle in her voice, "your bean soup is delicious. But we're going to pay for this tonight. It's too cold to leave the windows open, and you know what bean soup does to your tummy."

7

What does a cloud taste like?

"Do you think she was hatched from an egg? Or do you think she was... you know... born the normal way?"

"How on earth would I know?" muttered Wilson. She cast a warning look at Errol. "And, no, you're *not* going to ask her!"

"Why not?" Errol wanted to know, looking quite taken aback.

Wilson and Errol were sitting on their usual patch of grass next to the lake. It was a lovely sunny winter's day. They'd walked there together – and all the way Wilson had to listen to the thousands of new questions Errol had apparently thought up during the night.

Wilson looked at her watch. There was still no sign of Ava.

Fortunately, it was the school holidays, or she

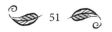

wouldn't have been able to come to the lake with Errol that morning. Her mum was a strict homeschool teacher. During the term she made sure that Wilson stuck to normal school hours.

A bee came slowly buzzing by.

"Did you know that honeybees have to visit four million flowers to make one kilogram of honey?"

Wilson and Errol both looked up. Ava was good at appearing out of the blue, without you even hearing her. Today she was wearing jeans with an embroidered floral pattern on one leg, a pair of bright white trainers and the same green jumper from yesterday.

"Four *million* flowers?" asked Errol.

Ava nodded. "Ma Zelna always tells people that when they complain about honey being expensive."

Errol cleared his throat. "Ava, can I ask you something?"

Ava nodded.

"Were you ha—"

"Would you like to do something?" Wilson quickly interrupted him. She shot Errol a look to make it clear that she wasn't going to allow him to ask stupid questions about eggs. "I mean, something nice – with us."

Ava smiled. "That sounds like fun. What do you have in mind?"

Wilson looked inquiringly at Errol. As far as she

knew, he'd lived in Leseeba all his life. He should know what they could do around here.

Errol's eyes lit up. "Do you want to go rowing on the lake?" he asked. "I know where we can find a boat."

Wilson wanted to object – she had never rowed in her life, and she just knew her mum wouldn't like the idea at all – but Ava looked very excited.

"That sounds fantastic!" she exclaimed.

Errol gestured for them to follow him. They made their way around the lake. In places the ground was wet, and Wilson had to be careful that her trainers didn't lose their grip on the slippery clay.

"My cousins sometimes go fishing here," said Errol over his shoulder. "They've invited me along a couple of times."

They walked quite a distance before Errol ducked into the trees. He stopped at a trunk that was blocking the path. It looked as if the massive old tree had fallen over many years ago. The trunk was covered in moss. Errol nimbly hopped over it. "You guys will have to come and help me," he said.

There was a small rowing boat with two oars inside hidden behind the tree trunk. Wilson looked at the boat doubtfully. The green paint was peeling off in places, and it had several holes that had been fixed with what looked suspiciously like bubble gum.

"I'm not getting into that thing," she declared. "We'll drown like rats."

Errol laughed. "Don't be such a scaredy-cat, Wilson. It's totally safe. I know what I'm doing."

"Hmph," snorted Wilson, but she picked up one side of the rowing boat with Ava.

Errol picked up the other side and they hoisted the little boat over the tree trunk. Huffing and puffing, they carried it to the water. Errol pulled off his trainers and socks and dragged the boat over the slippery clay into the shallows.

"Come on," he said to Wilson and Ava. "What are you waiting for?"

The two girls took off their trainers. When Ava pulled off her socks, Wilson couldn't resist the temptation to sneak a glance at her feet. She immediately felt silly. Ava had completely normal feet. What did she expect – bird claws?

Wilson shivered when she stepped into the water. The mud between her toes was cold and slimy.

"Errol Abrahams, if this boat sinks, you'd better hope that a big fish gobbles you up," she muttered.

Ava laughed that bright bell-like laugh of hers again. Errol held the boat steady for the girls to climb in. It was rocking dangerously, and Wilson and Ava sat down on the front bench as quickly as possible. Errol nimbly jumped aboard and nudged the boat away from the shore with an oar. He started rowing with long, smooth strokes.

"Not too far from the shore," Wilson warned.

Errol smiled in reply. Fortunately, he did seem to know what he was doing. The oars sliced rhythmically through the water.

Wilson could feel herself starting to relax.

Ava didn't look worried in the least. In fact, she appeared to be in seventh heaven. She leant back on the bench, smiled broadly, and closed her eyes. The bright winter sun made her skin glow like honey. She remained sitting like that for quite a while.

Keyyyyy-keyyy-keyyy-keyyy!

A strange bird call made Wilson frown.

"Fish eagle," said Errol. "It's beautiful, isn't it?"

Wilson was glad he hadn't brought his bird book along because she didn't feel like arguing about whether, in fact, a fish eagle's call *did* sound like that. Maybe he was right for once.

Errol stopped rowing so he could catch his breath. They drifted on the water. Errol leant back, like Ava, and stared up at the sky. But, unlike Ava, he couldn't keep quiet for much longer than a second.

"Have you ever wondered what a cloud tastes like?" he asked.

Wilson and Ava looked at each other and rolled their eyes. Then they burst out laughing.

"Hey, why are you guys laughing?" Errol asked indignantly. "Haven't you ever wondered about that?" He pointed up at the cotton clouds drifting by over their heads. "I think those clouds taste like egg white that's been whipped stiff, like sometimes when my grandma makes meringue."

Wilson shot him a warning glance. Was he really going to start talking about eggs again?

Ava played along. "I think thunder clouds taste like sour worms."

"And… rain clouds taste like… erm…" tried Wilson. "Oh, I don't know!" She gave up. "How many bizarre questions are living inside that head of yours, Errol?"

Errol grinned and shrugged.

Ava closed her eyes again and turned her face towards the sun. "What did you want to ask me earlier, Errol?"

Errol didn't wait to be invited twice. "Were you hatched from—"

Wilson glared at him again.

Ava opened her eyes and sat up.

"I think I know what the two of you want to know," she said.

"Hey, who said that I wanted to…" Wilson started protesting, but stopped when she saw what Ava was doing.

Ava sat up straight and pulled off her jumper. Wilson and Errol watched in silence. She was struggling a little because the jumper kept getting stuck behind her back. Then it slipped over her head with a *grrrrt* sound.

Fwwwp.

Wilson gulped.

"I don't believe it," whispered Errol.

Behind Ava's back two grey-brown wings were emerging. They were as long as her arms. The feathers were arranged in perfect rows. She stretched out her wings… *fwwwp…* and Wilson could feel a rush of air around her ears.

Now that Ava had taken off her jumper, she was wearing only a light grey sleeveless top. Her shoulders and arms were covered in perfect little feathers.

Ava lowered her eyes. "So," she said in a whisper, "now you know. They are hideous, aren't they?"

Wilson had to swallow a couple of times before she got her voice back. "Hideous?" she murmured. "Ava, they're not hideous at all. They're the most incredible thing I've ever seen." She stared in awe at the banded pattern on the feathers and reached out her hand to touch it. Ava flinched slightly, but allowed Wilson to gently caress the feathers. The feathers were soft and warm, and they rustled with a whispering sound under her fingertips.

"Can you fly?" Errol couldn't help himself. "Do you sleep in a nest at night? Were you hatched from an—"

"Ava!"

A loud, shrill voice came shooting over the water like an arrow, shattering the moment.

Ava's eyes widened in fear, and she snapped her wings closed.

A woman was standing on the bank of the lake. Even from a distance, Wilson could see by her stance how upset she was – an angry chin, square shoulders, hands on her hips.

"Ma Zelna," said Ava in a hoarse voice before Wilson could ask.

"Ava, come back!" ordered the voice. "Immediately."

Errol shot Ava an inquiring look, as if he was asking her permission. She nodded without saying a word.

With rhythmic strokes Errol started rowing.

Wilson's heart was pounding as they approached the figure at the edge of the water. Ava sat with her head hanging low, staring at the bottom of the rowing boat. The woman on the bank of the lake had flaming red hair. The look in her blazing eyes made Wilson wish Errol would turn the nose of the boat around and row to the other side instead.

When they'd almost reached the bank, the woman waded into the water without even taking off her boots. Impatiently, she dragged the boat to the shore.

"Ava! What's come over you? Who on earth are these children?"

As she spoke, the woman grabbed the green jumper. It looked as if Ava was going to get tangled up in it as the woman hurriedly put it back on.

"Has anyone else seen you?" she asked, sounding worried.

Before Ava could reply, the woman had already hauled her out of the boat.

"I'm sorry…" Wilson started stuttering. "We didn't…"

But the red-haired woman ignored her. She just stood there, waiting impatiently while Ava put her trainers on. Ava flashed an apologetic glance over her shoulder as she was marched away. Just as they were about to disappear among the trees, the redhead stopped short. She wheeled around and shot an icy look at Wilson and Errol.

"Not a word about this to anyone," she said. "Do you understand? Not a *word*."

8

The two mums

For the rest of the day Wilson couldn't shake the feeling she was knee-deep in trouble. But she wasn't sure exactly what kind of trouble it was.

After Ava left, she and Errol hauled the boat back up to its hiding place and walked back to town. Of course, Errol asked plenty of questions.

"Do you think Ava's two mums also have wings?"

"Do you think it's ticklish, having feathers on your arms?"

"Do you think that Ma Zelna woman knows who we are and where we live?"

"Do you think she's going to lock Ava up in a tower somewhere and throw the key away?"

"Do you think Ava's other mum is nicer?"

"Do you think Ava can bathe like a normal person? And what happens when her feathers get wet?

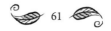

ERROL!

Or do you think she bathes in the dust, like a sparrow?"

It all became too much for Wilson.

"Errol, stop that!" she shouted when they were close to the caravan park. "All I'm hearing is *do-you-think-do-you-think-do-you-think*. Do you really *think* I can *think* about any of your questions if you don't stop talking for one single second?"

Errol must have been hurt by her outburst because he just muttered "Sorry" and headed home.

Wilson felt bad.

But there was one question she would have liked to ask *Errol*, even though he wouldn't know the answer any more than she did.

Do you think we'll ever see her again?

Late that afternoon there was a knock on the door of the Doll's House.

Wilson felt her stomach tighten. She knew immediately that the trouble she'd been expecting all day had just arrived.

Gabriel opened the door. Her mum was still at the tennis court.

"Afternoon, sir." It was Errol's voice. He sounded weird – a little formal. "Is… erm… is Wilson home?"

"Wils—" Gabriel started calling but she was already by his side.

Wilson gulped when she saw who was standing there. Errol wasn't alone. There were two women with him. One had soft blue eyes, a soft smile and hair that curled softly over her shoulders. The other had red hair and green eyes. Nothing about her looked soft.

"Are you Wilson?" asked the woman with the soft eyes. Her voice matched the rest of her – it wasn't soft, but it was friendly and warm.

Wilson nodded.

"Could we please have a word with you?"

Wilson felt Gabriel's eyes boring into her.

"Is Wilson in trouble?" he asked.

The woman smiled. "No, not at all," she said. "We need help from her and Errol. Could we maybe sit and talk somewhere? We won't be long."

Wilson nodded. She pointed to the camping chairs outside under the canopy. Gabriel was still standing in the doorway, watching them, a concerned look on his face.

"It's okay, Gabriel," said Wilson. "The ladies want us to help them find their… erm… lost parrot."

She could feel the colour rise in her face at the lie.

"Oh," said Gabriel. "Okay. Good luck, I hope you find it soon. I'll also keep my eyes peeled."

"Parrot?" Errol whispered as Gabriel closed the

door of the Doll's House. "*Really*?" But he stopped talking when the red-haired woman looked in his direction.

The two women cleared their throats.

"I'm sorry about this morning," said the woman with the red hair. "I shouldn't have been so… I got a terrible fright. Ava was irresponsible. If people found out about her… I'm sure you understand what would happen. It will ruin her life."

Suddenly her green eyes were no longer shooting arrows; they were pleading.

"But you can't keep her locked up forever," said Wilson.

"We don't keep her locked up!" said Ma Zelna. "Where did you get that from?"

The other woman – Rita, Wilson assumed – sighed. "Ever since Ava was a little girl, Zelna and I have tried to protect her. The world is a dangerous place for a special girl like her. Over the past few months, she has become careless. People have seen her. It's been in the local newspaper – twice."

Before Wilson could think of something to say, Errol breathed in sharply, the way he always did before asking a question.

"Can we still see her?"

Wilson could hardly believe her ears. For once, Errol had asked a *good* question!

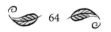

Ava's two mums looked at each other. It was a complex kind of look. Wilson could see that they were scared and worried and upset, all at once.

"I think it'll do her good," said Rita. "She misses other people. The two of us are all she's ever had."

"It's too dangerous," said Zelna.

"They already know her secret, and they haven't told anyone."

"Not *yet*."

Silence. Then Zelna turned to Wilson and Errol.

"She's not allowed to take off her jumper. Or go anywhere near the town. Do you understand?" Zelna tried to look stern, but there was a concerned tone to her voice that made it impossible for Wilson not to like her.

"Please," said Rita, "promise us that we can trust you."

When the two mothers left a few minutes later, Wilson stared after them.

"Do you trust *them*?" asked Errol. There was a strange sound in his voice.

Wilson wasn't sure what he meant. But before she could ask, Gabriel peeped out of the door of the Doll's House. "Is everything okay?"

Wilson didn't know how to answer that.

9

Biscuits and honey

"Erm… you have honey on the end of your nose, Errol," sniggered Ava.

Errol looked squint-eyed at the blob of honey on the tip of his nose. He tried to lick it off with his tongue and looked so funny in the process that both Wilson and Ava started to laugh.

It was a windy morning. The water in the lake was as dull and grey as lead. Wilson was wearing her thickest jacket, with a wool beanie on her head. She and Errol hadn't been sure they would find Ava at the lake again. But when they'd got there, she was already sitting in their usual spot beside the water, waiting for them. She'd brought them some biscuits and a jar of honey – and Errol needed no invitation. He tucked in greedily.

"I'm sorry about yesterday," said Ava. "About Ma Zelna making such a scene. And about her and Ma Rita coming to speak to you guys…"

Wilson and Errol looked at each other.

"We didn't mind," said Wilson slowly. "They were scared… you know… that more people would find out about…" She pointed at Ava's green jumper. "You know… about you."

Ava merely nodded. She drizzled a little more honey on a biscuit. "What does it feel like to live in a new place every couple of months, Wilson?" she asked, stuffing the whole biscuit into her mouth.

Wilson thought for a moment. "Well… I miss having a decent bedroom, one with real walls and a bed that you don't have to fold up every morning so that you have enough space to get dressed. And I miss going to a real school and having friends and…"

Wilson swallowed the rest of her sentence. She suddenly felt stupid. Ava had never been to a real school either, and she would never be able to go to one. And friends? Her two mums were the only other people she'd known her entire life.

"I'd love to stay in a different place every few months," said Errol. "I've never even been to Cape Town. All I know is what my mum and dad tell me about Table Mountain and the harbour and places like that." He stared longingly at the last biscuit in the packet.

Ava noticed and held the packet out to him. Drizzling a big blob of honey on it, he asked, "Wilson, you said that Gabriel's your stepfather. So, where's your real dad?"

Wilson felt a horrible hot knot in the pit of her stomach. Errol and his endless questions! But it felt kind of unfair not to answer. After all, Ava had shared *her* secret with them…

"He lives overseas," she muttered. "The last time I saw him was two years ago. But we chat sometimes. He lives in an ordinary house, with his new family, and as soon as things settle down, I'm going to go live with them."

"Oh," said Errol. "And you, Ava, what about—"

"Errol!" Wilson exclaimed. "That's none of your business."

"Okay, okay!" said Errol. "Sorry."

Ava shook her head. "It's okay," she said. She twisted the lid back on the honey jar. "I never knew my parents," she said without looking at Errol and Wilson. "My mum died when I was born and my dad…" She shrugged. "He was never in the picture. I don't even know who he is."

"Wow, really?" said Errol. "Wouldn't it be great if you could trace him?"

Wilson wished with all her heart that Ava would open the honey jar again and tip what was left over Errol's head.

But Ava just smiled, a slightly sad little smile.

"Ma Zelna and Ma Rita are incredible," she said. "They had to give up so much to raise me. The circus—"

"The circus?" This time it was Wilson who couldn't help asking.

Ava nodded. "Yep. Years ago, they were both working at a circus. Ma Rita trained horses – they called her the Horse Whisperer. Ma Zelna was a fire breather."

"No surprise to me," mumbled Errol. "She looked like she could spit fire yesterday."

Ava grinned. "That's where they got to know my mum. After my birth and my mum's death, they had to leave the circus to be able to raise me. Ma Rita loves animals – that's why she decided they should become farmers. She has a way with bees too. And

Ma Zelna puts her fire-breathing skills to good use by making smoke to calm the bees when they take out the honey!"

Wilson's head was spinning. A circus? A horse trainer and a fire breather? Ava's life was stranger than she could ever have guessed.

"Did your mum also... you know?" Errol pointed at the hump behind Ava's back and made flapping movements with his hands.

"Did she also have wings?" Ava laughed. "I don't mind you asking! No, my mum was... normal. She was a trapeze artist. Ma Zelna and Ma Rita say she was very good. They say she made it look as if she could fly."

"And you?" asked Errol. "Can you... fly?"

Ava stood up and started pulling her jumper over her head.

"Ava, your mums said you weren't allowed to do that!" protested Wilson.

But Ava ignored her. She dropped the green jumper on the ground.

Fwwwp.

She spread her wings.

It took Wilson's breath away to see the perfect grey-brown wings unfurl on either side of the girl's shoulders.

Ava ran to the nearest tree.

Fwwwp-fwwwp-fwwwp.

Wilson watched dumbfounded as the bird girl

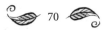

started flapping up the tree trunk. She wasn't flying… not exactly. Maybe her wings were too small to carry her full weight. But they helped her flutter-climb up the trunk in no time. On the first branch she squatted on her haunches and smiled down at Wilson and Errol. But suddenly the expression on her face changed. Her eyes widened.

At the same time Wilson heard a sound behind her. A twig snapping under the sole of a shoe.

Her breath froze in her throat.

Click.

She wheeled around.

"Gabriel, no!"

Before he could take another photo, Wilson was at his side. She made a grab for the camera, but Gabriel yanked it out of her reach.

"What are you doing?" Wilson shouted in dismay. "Why are you here? Did you follow us?"

Gabriel's eyes were glued to the girl in the tree.

"I… I… She has *wings*," he stammered.

"Give me the camera!" Wilson hissed. It felt as if the anger was burning her throat. "You have to delete that photo – immediately."

"Okay, okay!" said Gabriel. "Calm down, Wilson. I…" He looked completely gobsmacked. "Wilson, she has *wings*."

"That's none of your business, Gabriel. She's our friend. Don't you dare tell anyone about her."

Wilson's heart was racing after her outburst. Errol and Ava were watching her with large eyes. Neither of them said a word.

"Your mum asked me to keep an eye on you, Wilson," said Gabriel. "After those two women came by yesterday… we were worried that something was up."

"*Nothing* is up," said Wilson. "Ava is just… different. As you can see. That doesn't give you the right to take photos of her. Give me your camera!"

"It's fine, I don't mind."

Ava's voice came clear as a bell from up in the tree. Wilson gulped, astonished.

Fwwwp-fwwwp-fwwwp.

They stood in silence, watching as Ava flutter-climbed down to the ground. Gabriel's mouth was hanging open as Ava walked towards them. She stopped right in front of him and spread her wings with a challenging *fwwwp*. Gabriel recoiled slightly.

"Take more photos," said Ava.

"No!" Wilson shouted, horrified. "Don't, Ava. Your mums will—"

Ava looked at Wilson with a strange look in her eyes. "No one has ever taken a photo of me," she said. "Not even my mums. They're too scared."

Gabriel lowered his camera. "I can understand why," he said, suddenly looking concerned. "If someone got hold of photos of you…" His voice trailed off as he stared at Ava's wings, awestruck.

Wilson bit her lower lip. She couldn't help thinking of her mum's photo album. Wilson always moaned when her mum fetched the album to show complete strangers Wilson's baby photos. The fridge door in the Doll's House was also covered in images from her childhood. Wilson hated letting Gabriel take photos of her, but her mum loved it. What must it feel like not to have a single photo of yourself as a baby? Nor one of you, gap-toothed, on your first day of school? Nor one of a birthday or Christmas?

Gabriel was probably thinking of the same thing because he raised his camera again. "I'll print the photos at home and Wilson can give them to you. I'll delete them from my memory card. I promise."

Ava nodded and smiled.

Click. Click. Click.

"Hey, what about us?" asked Errol. "We also want to be in a photo with you."

"Yes, please!" said Ava.

Wilson and Errol positioned themselves on either side of her. Wilson wrapped her arm around Ava's shoulder. Between Ava's wings, the feathers on her back were soft and warm.

"Cheese!" Errol grinned.

Click.

Gabriel lowered his camera.

"You're only going to print *one* set of photos," said Wilson. "*Only* one set. And then you're going to delete them all."

Gabriel nodded meekly.

It looked as if his brain was still trying to comprehend what he had seen.

10
A head like a fish bowl

That afternoon, Wilson was lying on her bed, staring at the ceiling of the Doll's House. Her head felt like a fish bowl with far too many fish in it. They were milling about, and she was almost too scared to stick her hand into the bowl to try to grab one.

There was a gentle tap on her door and a moment later Gabriel peeped in.

"Are you okay?" he asked.

"Yes," muttered Wilson. "Why wouldn't I be?"

Gabriel sighed. "I've printed the photos. Will you give them to her?" He handed her a brown envelope. Wilson opened it.

Gabriel actually wasn't a bad photographer. What a pity he'd wasted his talent taking random photos for so many years. The photos of Ava were beautiful. There was one of her sitting up in the tree, and three of her looking directly at the camera, her arms folded. The last one was of Errol, Ava and Wilson. Wilson was the only one who was not smiling broadly at the camera.

"Are you sure you didn't print more?" asked Wilson. "And did you delete them all from your camera?"

Gabriel nodded. "I promise."

"Are you planning on telling my mum about this?" asked Wilson.

Gabriel looked awkward and studied his fingernails. "Your mum and I don't keep secrets from each other, Wilson…"

"Please, just this once?" She didn't like begging, but she wasn't sure how her mum would react to the news that her daughter had made friends with a girl who looked like a character from a video game.

"Okay, okay, I won't say anything," sighed Gabriel.

"Thanks." Wilson put the envelope and the photos on her bed. After Gabriel had left, she picked them up and looked at them again. If a journalist were to get hold of these and sell them to a newspaper or post them online…

One of the thought fish in Wilson's head suddenly leapt out of the fishbowl.

A newspaper.

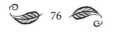

Something Rita had said the day before suddenly bothered her.

People have seen her. It's been in the local newspaper – twice.

Twice. Errol had only shown her one article. What did the other one say?

Wilson jumped up. She slipped the photos back into the envelope and put it in her backpack.

"I'm going to Errol's!" she called from the door of the Doll's House. Before Gabriel could reply, she was gone.

Wilson had never been to Errol's grandma's house, but she knew that it was the one with the red garden gate and the corrugated-iron roof over the porch. She pushed the gate open and walked up the narrow steps to the front door. She knocked and waited.

A few moments later, the door opened. A short old lady with grey hair and thick glasses greeted her with a friendly smile.

"Good afternoon?" she said with a question mark in her voice.

"Hello Mrs Abrahams," said Wilson. "Is Errol home?"

Granny Betty shook her head. "No, dear, he went out again after lunch. Come the holidays, he's always out in the streets. He said he was going to the show-grounds, to that funfair place."

"Oh." Wilson was surprised to find herself feeling slightly annoyed that Errol hadn't invited her to go to the funfair with him. After all, he knew she hadn't been yet. "Erm… thanks," she said.

She turned and started down the steps, but then she stopped and turned around.

"Wait!"

Granny Betty opened the door again. "Yes, dear?"

Another of the weird fish in Wilson's head had unexpectedly jumped out of the water.

"Do you know if Errol took his binoculars and bird book along?" she asked.

Granny Betty frowned. "Binoculars? No, my dear. Where would he get something like that?"

Wilson tried to ignore the uneasy feeling growing inside her. "Oh… erm… sorry, it was probably just a misunderstanding."

She turned and walked off before Granny Betty could ask any further questions. After she had closed the garden gate behind her, she stood in the street, for a moment unsure what to do.

Errol had told her that he'd brought his *dad's* binoculars when he came to fetch her to go birdwatching with him. But, immediately afterwards, he'd told Captain Calitz that they belonged to his *grandma*. And now his grandma didn't even know he *had* binoculars. So, why did he lie?

Wilson tried to collect her thoughts. The newspaper articles – that was why she'd come looking for Errol in the first place. Well, forget about Errol. For all she cared, he could hang out on his own at the funfair. Just then, Wilson knew where she could get hold of the newspaper articles.

11

Hush!

The glass door to the library sighed forlornly when Wilson pushed it open.

Inside, the building was dead silent – a musty, dusty kind of silence.

Wilson looked around. There seemed to be no one else in the library. She walked to the counter and cleared her throat.

"Erm… hello?"

A tall thin woman appeared from behind one of the bookcases carrying a pile of books in her hands. She sucked in her cheeks as if she'd just eaten a particularly sour sweet and glowered at Wilson over her glasses.

"There's no need to shout."

"I didn't…" Wilson started, but then decided it would be better to try to stay in the librarian's good books. "I didn't mean to shout. Sorry."

Miss Hannah looked just as strict as Errol had

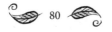

said. She wrinkled her nose as if smelling something bad.

"I've never seen you before. Do you live in this town?"

Wilson shook her head, then said, "Well, yes, for a while. We live in a motorhome, in the—"

"Sorry," said the librarian. "Unfortunately, without a permanent address I cannot issue you with a library card. And without a library card you cannot borrow books."

Except if your name is Errol Abrahams, Wilson thought, but of course she didn't say that.

"I'm actually only looking for a newspaper article," said Wilson. "Do you maybe keep old papers here?"

"Yes, of course we do," said the librarian. She sounded irritated. "What kind of library doesn't have newspapers? What newspaper are you looking for?"

"Erm… the local paper?" Wilson asked hesitantly.

The librarian nodded. "*The Postbox.* We have back issues in the archive."

"Erm… Could I maybe look at the ones from the last two or three months?" asked Wilson. "Please?"

"Sit here," said the librarian, pointing at a table. She placed her pile of books

on the counter and disappeared into a small room. A few moments later, she returned with a thick stack of newspapers. She plonked them down in front of Wilson. "Please turn the pages carefully. And if you tear anything out of one of the newspapers, there will be consequences."

She wrung her bony hands together threateningly.

Wilson gulped. "All right," she said.

She opened the file and looked at the date on the top newspaper. It was that week's issue. The paper wasn't very thick. Wilson started paging through the issues, her eyes flying over the headlines.

Ina's milk tart wins first prize again!
Cowboy dance in aid of old-age home
More garden gnomes go missing
Captain Calitz's top tips for pruning roses
Leseeba children excel on rugby field

In the issue of two weeks ago, on page three, Wilson found the article Errol had shown her.

She began to page through earlier issues. Then, just as her eyes were starting to go blurry, she found it. The other article had appeared more than a month ago.

LESEEBA

WEEKLY NEWSPAPER

THE POSTBOX

{FREE}

ISSUE: 784

CHILDREN CLAIM TO HAVE SEEN STRANGE "BIRD GIRL"

Three children who went fishing this past weekend claim that they saw a peculiar "bird girl".

Brothers Almero (15) and Denver (14) Abrahams, and their cousin Errol (12), were in a rowing boat on the town lake when they spotted a figure among the reeds.

"It looked like a girl," Errol told the editorial staff of *The Postbox*, "but she had wings like a bird."

His two cousins apparently also saw something among the reeds, but they weren't sure what it was. "It looked like a girl," said Almero, "but it could also have been a big goose or something."

"We don't want people to laugh at us," added Denver.

Captain Chester Calitz, the head of the police, said children should rather not go fishing on their own at the town lake. He wouldn't comment on the children's claims about the "bird girl".

Wilson sat up straight.

"What the…" she muttered, lost in thought.

"Hush!" hissed Miss Hannah.

Wilson looked around and raised an eyebrow at the librarian. "Why do I need to keep quiet?" she whispered. "There's no one else in the library. And no wonder – I've been in many libraries, but I've never been in one this dull and boring and unimaginative. A library is supposed to be a place full of... full of surprises and cheerful things."

Husssh!!

As Miss Hannah started to protest, Wilson turned around and left the library.

Outside, the winter sky was grey and the afternoon sun shone weakly on the parched yellow lawn in front of the library. Wilson was wondering what to do next. Should she go and look for Errol at the funfair?

But then something strange happened. A canary-yellow van came driving by. Then it stopped, and the back door opened.

Wilson's eyes widened. Errol got out!

When the van drove off, he saw her too.

"Hey, Wilson!" he called.

Wilson slung her backpack over her shoulders and marched over to him.

"I thought you were at the funfair," she said. "That's what your gran said."

"Oh... erm... were you looking for me?" asked Errol, raising his eyebrows.

Wilson nodded.

"I *was* at the funfair. Mr Leo Faber had… erm… some odd jobs for me to do."

"Mr Faber?" Wilson asked with a frown.

"Yep," said Errol. "He's the owner of the funfair. I've been helping him for the past few days… you know, putting up posters, stuff like that. For pocket money."

"Oh," said Wilson, trying her best not to sound hurt. After all, it was none of her business if he wanted to earn money at the funfair; he didn't have to tell her about it. It wasn't as if they were really *friends* or anything.

But there *was* something that he *should* have told her…

"Why didn't you tell me that you were in the newspaper?" she asked. "The first time you saw Ava was more than a month ago."

Errol kicked at the kerb with the tip of his trainer

and looked down. "I didn't want you to think that I was nuts," he mumbled. "You won't believe how the other kids teased my cousins and me after that story came out!"

"But even *after* we'd seen Ava, you didn't tell me!" said Wilson.

Errol shrugged. "I didn't really think about it. Sorry!"

Wilson slowly breathed out. "That's okay," she said.

Errol smiled, looking relieved.

"So, can we go and look for Ava again tomorrow?" asked Wilson. "I want to give her the photos that Gabriel printed."

"Did Gabriel give them to you?" Errol asked excitedly.

Wilson nodded and took the envelope out of her backpack.

Tilting his head, Errol flipped through the photos Wilson had handed him. He grinned when he saw the one of the three of them together.

"Do you always look that grumpy in photos, Wilson?" he asked.

Wilson stuck her tongue out at him.

Errol cleared his throat as Wilson took the photos, slipped them back into the envelope and returned it to her backpack. "Erm... listen, Wilson..." he said. "Mr Faber gave me complimentary tickets to the funfair. If you don't have any other plans, we can go together."

Wilson thought for a moment. She *did* tell Gabriel that she was going to Errol's – she just didn't say that they were going to the funfair.

"Okay," she said, "as long as I'm home before dark."

12
The funfair

The name of the funfair was written in huge colourful letters over the entrance: FUN LAND.

Above the sound of the cheerful carnival music, you could hear children laughing and yelling.

Fun Land did not look as impressive as the funfairs Wilson had seen before, but there was still a lot to do. There was a big wheel with revolving seats, a merry-go-round with different animals to ride, a ghost train, an octopus with arms that spun round and round, a ride with swings hanging from long chains, and various stalls where you could play games to win prizes.

Errol's eyes were shining with excitement as he looked at the different rides. "What do you want to try first?" he asked Wilson. "We can go on all the rides for free, but we have to pay for the stalls."

"How about the big wheel?" suggested Wilson.

"Perfect!" said Errol.

A short line of people were waiting to get on the big wheel. Wilson and Errol joined the queue. When they reached the front of the line, Errol pulled two tickets from his back pocket and showed them to the attendant. The woman took a quick look at the tickets and nodded. Then she helped them into their seats and made sure that they were buckled in properly.

Wilson's stomach gave a slight lurch when the wheel started to move. From below, the wheel didn't really look all that high, but when they were at the top the ground suddenly looked very far away.

"Look," said Errol, "you can see the whole town from here."

Wilson's eyes wandered over the houses and trees. On the other side she saw the trees in the caravan park, but she couldn't spot the Doll's House. A short distance beyond the houses, the lake was glittering in the afternoon light.

Errol squeezed his eyes shut and held his hands in the air when they started the steep descent. "Whoopeee!" he screamed. "It feels like I'm flying!"

Wilson did the same. Well, except for the "Whoopeee!" part. Wilson was quite sure she had never in her entire life screamed "Whoopeeee!" and she wasn't about to start anytime soon.

The afternoon air was icy cold against her cheeks. Errol was right. If Ava could use her wings to fly long distances, she thought, it would feel just like this.

After riding the big wheel, they tried every single ride at the funfair. They  didn't have to pay for any of them – Errol just showed the complimentary tickets the owner of the funfair had given him. The swings were a bit wild – Wilson felt slightly queasy when they got off. At the merry-go-round she chose a dolphin and Errol chose a donkey. Wilson was terribly embarrassed because he kept hee-hawing as they went round and round. The ghost train made Wilson roll her eyes quite a few times. Only a three-year-old would be spooked by the ghosts and mummies and werewolves, which all looked just like mannequins in bad Halloween costumes.

When dusk began to fall, Wilson looked at her watch.

"I have to go home," she said.

"Or my mum and Gabriel will be worried."

"Just one more!" pleaded Errol. "Look!"

He pointed to a stall where you had to use a big hammer to hit a red button as hard as you could. A small ball shot up a pole to show how hard you had struck the button.

"I didn't bring enough money," groaned Wilson. There were only a few coins in her backpack.

"Don't worry, I have money," said Errol.

Even though it was cold, the man at the stall was wearing a tank top. His muscular arms were full of tattoos. "So, buddy, you wanna show the girlie how strong you are?" he asked Errol in a gruff voice and winked.

Wilson wanted to tell the man that she wasn't a "girlie", but his size made her think twice. Errol paid the man and handed Wilson the hammer.

"No, you first," she said.

Errol struggled to pick up the hammer.

"You have three tries," said the man with the tattoos. He looked at Errol's small arms and chuckled.

Errol hit the red button.

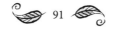

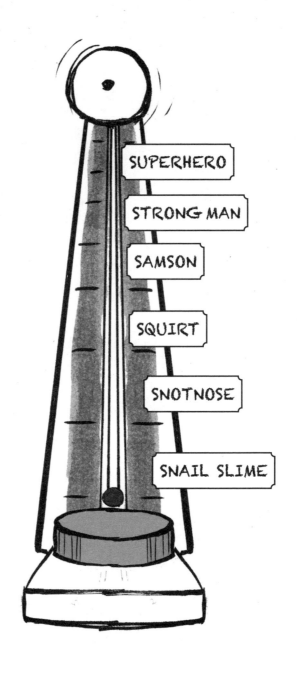

SUPERHERO

STRONG MAN

SAMSON

SQUIRT

SNOTNOSE

SNAIL SLIME

DWANG!

Wilson couldn't help laughing. The ball had only gone up to *SNAIL SLIME.*

"My hand slipped," Errol muttered.

With his next two attempts he managed to get up to *SNAIL SLIME* and *SNOTNOSE.*

"Your turn," he said to Wilson. "I can hold your backpack for you."

Wilson handed him her backpack and picked up the hammer. It was heavier than it looked.

DWANG!

The ball shot up to *SQUIRT.*

"Hmph," scoffed Errol. "That was just luck."

Wilson raised the hammer again.

DWANG!

SQUIRT.

"Seems like the girlie's arms are stronger than yours, buddy," said the man with the tattoos to Errol. "You'll have to eat more porridge."

Wilson raised the hammer again and hit the button as hard as she could.

DWANG!

The thud made her teeth chatter.

SAMSON!

"I'm impressed, girlie," said the man with the tattoos. "You could become a wrestler!"

It was Errol's turn to laugh.

"Maybe," muttered Wilson. "And when I'm a wrestler, I'll make sure everyone who ever called me girlie will be very sorry."

13
Gone

When Wilson opened one eye lazily the next morning, a sliver of sun was already falling through the narrow gap between her curtains. She immediately closed her eye and pulled the duvet up to her chin. She'd had multicolour funfair dreams all night.

Wilson smiled contentedly as she burrowed into her warm, cosy duvet nest. Yesterday afternoon had been great fun. The funfair had to have been one of the most exciting things to happen in Leseeba in a long time. She wished Ava could have experienced it with her and Errol. It must be terrible always having to hide and missing fun things because people might see who you really were.

Wilson pushed her duvet aside and sat up. She wondered whether they would see Ava later. Would she be at the lake again? Maybe she could give her the photos. She thought Ava would like them.

Wilson bent down and picked up her backpack. She opened it and rummaged around inside.

Her hand froze in shock.

She groped around again.

Then she yanked the backpack open and tipped everything out onto her bed.

It's gone.

The words shot through her brain like a double flash of lightning.

At first, she didn't want to believe what her eyes were seeing – or, rather, *not* seeing. She stared at the contents. A pencil, some coins, lots of sweet wrappers, a packet of gum, the complimentary funfair tickets that Errol had given her afterwards as a keepsake.

The envelope with the photos was gone.

Wilson flew out of bed.

"Gabriel!" She yanked the door open. "Gabriel, where are the photos?"

Gabriel was in the tiny kitchen, making coffee. He still looked half-asleep.

"What?" he mumbled. "What are you talking about?"

"Don't act stupid!" snapped Wilson. "The photos that you took of Ava!"

"Wilson!" Her mum's voice was as fast and sharp as a volley being whacked across the net. She walked out of their room, still in her pyjamas. "Since when do you speak to Gabriel like that?"

Wilson gasped in dismay. "Ava's. Photos. Are. Gone," she said.

Her mum frowned. "Who's Ava?"

Wilson gulped. Oops.

So, Gabriel had kept his word. He hadn't told her mum about the bird girl. Suddenly Wilson wished that he *had* rather. Because now she was the one who had to explain what was going on. How do you tell your mum that you'd met a girl with wings like a bird? And now she didn't even have the photos to prove she was telling the truth…

"Wilson has made friends with a girl who has wings," said Gabriel.

For a moment, you could hear a pin drop in the Doll's House.

"Wings?" her mum snorted.

Gabriel and Wilson nodded.

"Her name is Ava," said Wilson. "Gabriel took photos of her. Photos that *no one* else was supposed to see. And now they're gone."

There was a strange look in her mum's eyes. It looked as if she was wondering how on earth her husband and daughter could have lost their marbles at the same time.

But Wilson didn't feel like explaining. She suddenly thought of Jennifer Zeelie.

If you haven't heard of Jennifer Zeelie, it's Gabriel's fault. No, honestly.

Jennifer Zeelie was the reason he was the Most Hated Photographer on Earth *and* why he lost his job as a newspaper photographer.

Jennifer Zeelie was a young singer who'd taken part in a big talent competition on TV. *Stardust* was the name of the programme. People were crazy about her. Everyone thought she would win and become the country's next big pop star.

But then Gabriel found out that Jennifer's boy-friend, Brad Bailey, was the son of one of the judges on *Stardust*, and snuck a photo of the two of them partying together at a nightclub. It was published in the newspaper and people started claiming that Jennifer had an unfair advantage. Jennifer and Brad denied everything and said they'd run into each other by accident that night. Gabriel refused to believe them. He started following the two everywhere.

One weekend they went camping together in the Drakensberg. Gabriel tailed them and took a photo of them kissing on a hike. When they spotted him, Jennifer and Brad tried to flee from the camera. Jennifer was in such a rush that she wasn't paying attention to where she was going. Her foot slipped and she tumbled down a steep slope. Afterwards, the doctor said that she'd been lucky to have broken only an arm and a leg.

The next morning the headlines in the papers weren't *Young singer's boyfriend is son of Stardust judge.* They were *Photographer destroys young singer's career.* In a TV interview Brad Bailey lashed out at greedy paparazzi who had no respect for people's privacy and careers.

With her arm and leg in plaster, Jennifer no longer wanted to take part in the competition. She withdrew and someone else won. No one knew what happened to her afterwards.

The public was furious with Gabriel. People drew up petitions to demand his resignation, but before he could resign, the newspaper fired him.

And *that* was why Wilson was now glaring suspiciously at Gabriel.

"Did you steal those photos, Gabriel?" she asked. "That's what you do, after all, isn't it – *steal* photos? Did you change your mind and decide to sell Ava's photos? How much will they be worth? Probably more than a photo of a young singer and her boyfriend, don't you think?"

"Wilson!" Again, her mum whacked her name at her like a tennis ball. "This whole story sounds to me like a prank or a… scam. A girl with wings… something like that just cannot exist."

Rat-a-tat-tat!

A loud, urgent knock on the door.

Wilson wheeled around and opened it.

For a moment, she was too startled to say anything. Then she turned to her mother.

"If Ava doesn't really exist, tell her mums that. They're here."

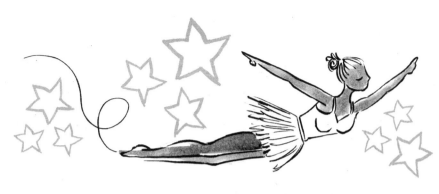

14
A fairy tale

"Are you sure she isn't here?" asked Rita.

Wilson raised an eyebrow. The Doll's House was so small that they could barely hide a canary in it, let alone a girl with wings.

"I don't understand," said Wilson's mother. "Is your daughter… missing?" She shot Gabriel an inquiring look. "I thought you said the two women had been here about a *parrot* that was missing!"

Wilson and Gabriel shared a guilty look.

"We're terribly worried," said Zelna. "She didn't sleep in her bed last night. If the wrong people… the wrong *person* gets hold of her…"

Wilson's mum clutched her head with both hands. "Will someone *please* tell me what exactly is going on here?" she groaned.

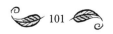

Rita and Zelna looked at each other. Together, they nodded.

"Maybe it's time we told you the full story," said Rita.

Gabriel pointed to the camping chairs under the canopy. "Take a seat," he said. "I'll bring us coffee and a hot cocoa for you, Wilson."

Wilson slipped inside to swap her pyjamas for jeans, a warm top and her trainers.

A few minutes later, when everyone was sitting outside, each with a mug that was steaming in the cold morning air, Rita started telling them Ava's story. Wilson listened, mesmerised. It sounded like a fairy tale. And the fairy tale went something like this...

Once upon a time there was a young woman who could fly. Well, not actually fly, no – but she was so dainty and light-footed that people gave her the nickname Birdie. She was an acrobat who took spectators' breath away when she soared through the air, or delicately balanced on a thin tightrope.

No one at Faber's Circus was sure exactly where she'd come from, because she spoke with a strange accent – the few times that she did speak – and her skin was the colour of honey.

Birdie was one of the stars of Faber's Circus. She was

even more popular than Zelna the fire breather, or Rita's
snow-white horses with the wavy plumes on their heads.
On the circus posters you could see her flying through
the air, tiny but fearless. Only the lions were more
popular, but everyone knows that lions are always the
most popular act in any circus. Night after night, Birdie
took people's breath away.

And then one day she simply disappeared. The ring-
master was distraught and frantic with worry – he looked
everywhere for his young star, but no one knew what had
happened to her. She'd disappeared as mysteriously as
she'd appeared at the circus.

Months went by. And then, one day, Birdie was back.

The ringmaster was furious. "Do you know how much
money I lost while you were away?" he roared. "If you
do that again, you're fired. You'd better be back on the
job tonight."

But everyone could see that
Birdie wouldn't be able to perform
right away. Zelna the fire breather
and Rita the horse whisperer
went to plead with the ring-
master. They took Birdie into their
care. A week later, she gave
birth to a baby.

The baby girl was healthy, a
screaming little bundle of joy.

"You must call her Ava," Birdie whispered to Zelna the fire breather and Rita the horse whisperer before she drew her last breath.

"We'll have to find someone to adopt the baby," the ringmaster grumbled when they went to share the news with him in his caravan. "The circus is already struggling. We can't feed extra mouths."

But when he saw the little baby, he instantly changed his mind.

"She belongs to the circus now," he said with a greedy gleam in his eyes. "And she's going to make us all stinking rich. She's going to be the star of Faber's Circus – much more famous than her mother."

The baby, you see, had wings. Pink stumpy wings covered in fine, fluffy yellow down, just like the down on her shoulders and arms. The fluffy little stumps flapped up and down when she cried or was hungry.

That evening Zelna the fire breather and Rita the horse whisperer, sitting with the sleeping bird baby, exchanged a worried look.

"We can't let her stay here," Zelna announced, with determination in her voice. "What kind of life would she have?"

Rita nodded, her eyes as soft as the eyes of her beloved horses, and smiled at the sleeping baby. "Faber will exhibit her like she's an object in a museum, like a freak of nature. We can't allow that."

That night the fire breather and the horse whisperer fled. Their circus days were over forever – and the circus's days were numbered too. The two women took with them the baby with the fluffy down wings that in time would grow into big, strong wings. They carried the baby far away from the circus, where they could raise her, hiding her wings from the world. And away from the greedy ringmaster, who would spend years and years searching for her, even when he no longer had a circus.

The story Wilson had just heard was so strange and fantastical and sad and exciting that it left her speechless, exactly as a good circus act should. The mug of cocoa in her hands had long since grown cold. She stared at Rita and Zelna as though she was seeing them for the very first time.

Something finally went *click* in her head, like a small cog shifting into place and, in turn, setting off a whole series of cogs.

"That name," she said.

Four pairs of eyes looked at her inquiringly.

But Wilson had already leapt to her feet. "I have to go speak to someone," she called over her shoulder.

15
No time for jokes

That morning Errol himself opened the door – not his grandma. It looked as if he hadn't brushed his hair yet, and there was a blob of toothpaste on the front of his T-shirt.

"Who is Mr Faber?" asked Wilson.

Errol frowned. "Good morning, Wilson. How're you? Did you sleep well? Please come—"

"Stop!" snapped Wilson. "This is no time for jokes. Who is Mr Faber?"

Errol shrugged. "I told you – the man who owns the funfair. What's—"

"What job are you doing for him?" demanded Wilson.

Wilson watched Errol intently. Was it her

imagination or did she, for a split second, see guilt flit across his face?

"I told you, didn't I? Putting up posters and handing out pamphlets, that kind of thing. Why do you want to—"

"Did he give you the binoculars?"

Errol glanced over his shoulder and stepped out onto the porch. He pulled the door closed behind him. "Softer," he whispered. "I don't want to get my gran in a flap. What are you talking about?"

"Don't act dumb," snapped Wilson. "The binoculars. Did Mr Faber give them to you? Did he ask you to keep an eye on Ava?"

Errol didn't reply and Wilson knew immediately what that meant.

"Errol, did you take the photos from my backpack?"

The question hung heavily in the air between them. Then, unexpectedly, tears welled up in Errol's eyes. He nodded. "Wilson, I… I'm sorry," he stammered. "I didn't mean to—"

"Do you realise what you have *done*?" shouted Wilson. "Ava's disappeared! Her mums don't know what's happened to her. She went missing last night. And Mr Faber from the funfair… he… I think he used to be a ringmaster. He's been looking for Ava for years."

"I know," said Errol.

Wilson couldn't believe what she was hearing.

"Then *why* did you help him find her?" The question shot out of Wilson's chest like a ball of fire, scorching her throat, as if she had suddenly mastered Zelna's famous circus act.

Errol swallowed hard. He looked down at his shoes. "Mr Faber is Ava's dad."

Wilson felt as though Errol had just struck her on the chest with the hammer from the funfair. She gasped for breath.

"That's… impossible."

Errol sat down on the low porch wall. He picked one of his grandma's dead geraniums and crushed the petals to powder between his fingers as he spoke.

"Mr Faber has indeed been looking for Ava ever since she was born. A few weeks ago, he saw the newspaper article on the internet, the one that mentioned my name. It was easy for him to trace me. He promised me a lot of money if I could find out where Ava lived, and he also gave me the binoculars."

Wilson sat next to him on the porch wall. The anger in her chest had suddenly been snuffed out. "Oh, Errol," she muttered. "I promised Ava she could *trust* you…"

Errol shook his head. "You don't understand. Granny Betty needs the money. She works her fingers to the bone to make clothes for people, but she still doesn't even make enough to buy herself new glasses. The optometrist said she needs an eye operation and that's very expensive… And my mum and dad work hard in Cape Town. They both have *two* jobs, but they don't earn enough to send us more than a few hundred rand every month, and they only come to visit once or twice a year…"

Wilson paused. "I'm sorry," she said. "But still. What you did wasn't right."

Errol gave Wilson an imploring look. "But this is Ava's dad, Wilson! Rita and Zelna aren't her real mums; they *kidnapped* her as a baby."

Wilson thought hard for a moment about what he'd said. "I don't know if that's true, but whether Mr Faber is Ava's real dad or not, I don't think he's a good man," she said.

"I think you're right," Errol admitted at last.

The cogs in Wilson's brain started turning again.

"I think we have to tell my mum and Gabriel what's going on, and Ava's mums. Maybe even Captain Calitz."

"Uurgh, Wilson." Errol's eyes were pleading desperately. "I'm going to get into big trouble if they find out what I've done. And what if the whole world finds out about Ava's wings? Please. I'll go to the funfair with you. Let's first go and see if we can find Ava ourselves."

Wilson thought quickly. Should she spill the beans, or should they try to find out on their own what had happened to Ava?

Wilson wasn't sure whether she could trust Errol but she said it anyway: "Okay."

"Thanks, Wilson, let me just put on some clean clothes," said Errol as he rushed inside.

16

A padlock

"And where are the two of you off to now?"

Wilson stopped dead in her tracks. How on earth did Captain Calitz always manage to appear on his bike like a ghost out of the blue?

"Morning, Captain!" said Errol, while Wilson grasped for words. "We're on our way to the funfair."

The policeman's moustache twitched slightly. "Hmph. I can't wait for that funfair to pack up and leave town. People who move from town to town like that mean only one thing – trouble."

"Wait a minute!" said Wilson. "What do you mean…"

Errol shot her a warning glance. Captain Calitz folded his arms as he waited to hear what she was going to say next.

"Forget it," she muttered.

"You should also come to the funfair, Captain," said Errol. "That big wheel is really high. It makes your tummy turn. And the swings are great fun too."

Wilson couldn't help wondering what Captain Calitz would look like on the back of one of the merry-go-round animals. Maybe the penguin. The picture in her head was so funny that she had to bite her bottom lip not to burst out laughing.

Captain Calitz's only response to this suggestion was "Hmph".

"Enjoy your day, Captain!" said Errol and started walking off.

Wilson followed him, relieved. Captain Calitz had a knack for always making her feel as if she had done something wrong.

The closer they got to the funfair, the more anxious Wilson felt. By the time they passed under the Fun Land sign, she thought she might faint.

"How on earth are we going to look for Ava, Errol?" she asked in a muffled voice. "We can't just snoop around for everyone to see."

Errol seemed quite calm. "Wilson, the secret is to look like you belong here. You can snoop around almost anywhere, and people will leave you alone – as long as you look as if you belong."

With a broad smile and a cheeky swagger, Errol walked on. He looked as if the place belonged to him. Wilson breathed out slowly and trailed behind him. She tried her best to follow his example but that was easier said than done. Errol might have looked as if he belonged there, but she probably looked as if she had come to rob the ticket office.

First, they wandered among the stalls. It was still early – none of the rides were operating yet and the stalls were deserted. There wasn't much going on at the row of caravans, either. Here and there a fire was burning, and in front of one of the caravans a woman was washing clothes in a metal bath.

"Errol, we can't just go poking around the caravans," whispered Wilson.

"We can," said Errol. "We simply have to look…"

"… as if we belong here," said Wilson. "Okay, fine."

Errol shoved his hands into his hoodie pockets. Whistling a jaunty tune, he walked past the woman who was doing the washing. He raised a hand and

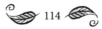

waved to her, and she waved back. "That smells good enough to eat!" he called to a man who was cooking eggs in a pan over an open fire.

The man gave him a gap-toothed smile and raised his thumb in the air.

Wilson could hardly believe what she was seeing. Errol was very good at this.

"That one over there," Errol said softly to Wilson. He gestured with his eyes towards a blue caravan that was parked away from the others, among some lorries and trailers.

Wilson nodded.

They walked straight past the blue caravan and then Errol silently snuck behind a big lorry. Wilson followed, her heart thumping against her ribcage.

Errol gestured for her to follow him as he wove in and out of the vehicles and trailers, until he had circled back to the blue caravan. Errol stood on his tiptoes and peered through the window.

"What do you see?" Wilson whispered.

"Nothing," replied Errol in a muffled voice. "The curtains are closed."

Wilson tried the next window.

Inside the dimly lit caravan, she couldn't make out much. A narrow strip of sunlight fell in through the curtains, illuminating a small green rug, a chair, a bed and...

She gasped.

"Errol!"

In a flash, he was by her side and clambering onto the wheel of the caravan to get a look. "It's her!" he said.

Ava was lying on the bed. She seemed to be asleep.

Tap-tap-tap.

Errol knocked on the window, the way he'd knocked on Wilson's window to wake her up.

Ava didn't stir.

TAP-TAP-TAP.

Errol knocked even louder.

No reaction.

"You think she's okay?" Wilson asked, worried. "Why isn't she waking up?"

Errol jumped off the wheel. Then he slipped round to the front of the caravan. Wilson hesitated for a moment before following him. She was sure someone was going to see them, and any second now they would shout, "Hey, what are those two kids doing here? Grab them!"

"It's locked from the outside," whispered Errol. He pointed at the door of the caravan. There was a big padlock hanging on the door.

Wilson's heart sank into her trainers. How on earth were they going to open it?

But Errol seemed to already have a plan. He slipped

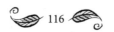 116

round the caravan again and jogged off towards the lorries and trailers. Wilson felt like a tail following Errol wherever he went, but she wasn't going to stay by the caravan on her own. If someone asked what they were doing there, Errol would hopefully be able to smooth-talk their way out of trouble.

Errol walked along the row of lorries and trailers, checking the back of every vehicle. Wilson didn't have the foggiest idea what he was looking for.

"Aha!" he hissed triumphantly. He leaned over the open back of a lorry and picked up something heavy.

Wilson frowned. "A sledgehammer?" she asked. "You can't be serious."

The hammer Errol was holding looked a lot like the one they had used to whack the button at the funfair stall.

"Do you have a better plan?" Errol asked.

Wilson raised an eyebrow. "Snail Slime. Snotnose," she said.

Errol pretended not to hear. He picked up the sledge-hammer and walked determinedly back to the blue caravan. He looked like some sort of mythological hammer-swinging hero. Wilson was sorry he couldn't see the impressive eye-roll she was doing behind his back.

Errol stopped at the door of the caravan. Wilson looked around nervously. Fortunately, luck seemed to be on their side. The woman who had been doing her washing was no longer there, and there was no one else in sight.

CLANG!

The sound was so loud and unexpected that Wilson jumped with fright.

The lock was still hanging on the caravan door.

Groaning, Errol raised the hammer again.

CLANG!

The padlock swayed slightly.

Wilson was getting very worried. How could Ava still be sleeping through all the noise?

With a muffled groan, Errol raised the hammer again.

CLANG!

Still nothing happened. There was a dent in the caravan door where the hammer had struck it.

"You missed," said Wilson. "Give me that."

Before Errol could protest, Wilson grabbed the hammer from him. It wasn't quite as heavy as the one they'd used the day before at the stall. Wilson took a step back, hoisted the hammer and focused her full attention on the padlock. She leant forward with her whole body and…

CLANG!

Clink.

The padlock fell to the ground.

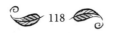

"Okay, okay," muttered Errol. "You win."

Wilson tried her best not to look smug but didn't quite succeed.

Errol yanked the caravan door open and peered inside. "Ava?" he called softly. "Are you here?"

Wilson pushed him aside and scrambled into the caravan. "Ava!" she hissed. "Ava, wake up!"

The little bundle on the bed stirred slightly.

Wilson opened the curtains.

Ava slowly opened her eyes and squinted in the sharp sunlight streaming in.

Errol had slipped into the caravan behind Wilson. "Ava, we've come to fetch you!" he whispered.

Ava looked confused, as if she wasn't quite sure where she was or who Wilson and Errol were.

"There was a man…" she said, sitting up. "He said… he said he was my real dad…"

"That's absolutely right," said a voice.

It was a gruff, lazy voice that sent icicles down Wilson's spine.

17
A golden birdcage

The man standing in the door of the caravan had a bushy mane of golden hair that fitted his name perfectly. Leo Faber was tall and stout, and he filled the entire doorway.

"Did the two of you come and visit my little birdie?" he asked.

Wilson took a step back. "You… you can't keep her locked up," she stammered.

One corner of the funfair owner's mouth turned up slightly. "No need to worry," he said. "I'm Ava's father – I've already explained that to you, haven't I, Errol? I thought you were

on my side, my boy. Ava isn't a prisoner… I only want to protect her."

"*Protect*?" Wilson spat out the word. "Then why was the door locked from the outside?"

Now the other side of the man's mouth turned up to form an uncomfortable smile. "All I wanted was to make sure no one took my little birdie away from me again. That's what happened years ago." He walked up to the bed and gently stroked the small feathers on Ava's shoulder. "Do you know how long I've been searching for you?"

Ava flinched slightly… but then she looked up at the man and smiled hesitantly. She rubbed her eyes and shook her head, as if she was trying to clear her mind.

"What's the matter with her?" Errol asked with a worried frown. "Why does it look like she can't wake up properly?"

"I gave her something to calm her down a little," said Leo Faber. "She got a terrible fright. But now she's safe."

Wilson shook her head. "No," she said. "She doesn't belong here. Ava, you must come home. Your mums… they're worried sick about you."

Ava's eye widened. "Ma Zelna… Ma Rita…" she whispered.

The owner of the funfair reached out and raised Ava's chin so that she could look him in the eye.

 121

"Ava, your life will never be the same," he said. "No one will ever try to hide you like some terrible secret again. You're a special, special child, and it's time to show you off to the world."

"*No!*" Wilson exclaimed again, this time so loudly that her voice echoed through the caravan. "She's not a… a freak that you can take from town to town and make people pay to look at."

Leo Faber's head snapped around, his tawny eyes drilling into Wilson's. "Of course, people are going to pay to see her!" he roared so forcefully that Wilson took a step back in fright. "They're going to pay so much money. She's going to travel with the funfair and get her own act. I'm going to have a golden cage made for her and she will perform inside it. Ava is going to be world-famous. I'll make sure she gets the special life that someone like her deserves. And no one will stop me!" Suddenly, he seemed embarrassed by his outburst. He went back to stroking the feathers on Ava's shoulder. "Ava's days of being hidden away are over. You two can go and tell her so-called mums that. If they try to interfere again, I'm going to show the world her photo anyway. Do you understand?"

Wilson's heart tightened. The photos! She had completely forgotten about them.

On the bed Ava made a faint squeak. Then she whispered, almost inaudibly, "I want to go home."

"But you *are* home," said Leo Faber. "The circus was your home from the day you were born, and now the funfair is your home."

Ava shook her head. The fog seemed to be lifting from her mind.

"Ma Zelna!" she called out. "Ma Rita!"

"Ava!" Leo Faber bent over her, but Ava leapt up unexpectedly. Her wings shot open.

Fwwwp.

Cold air rushed past Wilson's face. The owner of the funfair staggered back, his mouth open. Ava leapt forward and shoved him aside with an angry yell. His eyes widened… and he lost his balance. With a roar, he tumbled out the caravan door.

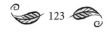

Ava didn't hesitate for one second. She shot forward. In a flash she was out of the caravan. Wilson felt Errol grab her hand and yank her forward. Her legs started moving by themselves, even though her brain felt paralysed.

She was running.

She heard people screaming and a man bellowing furiously behind her.

But she looked neither left nor right.

She kept running.

Errol and Ava were next to her. She could hear them panting, and the flap-flapping of Ava's wings, which seemed to drive her forward even faster.

They zigzagged between the lorries and trailers, past rows of empty horse stables, scrambled over a fence and weaved in and out of the bushes and trees. It felt like an eternity before they finally came to a halt. Wilson couldn't run any more. Her chest was on fire. She looked around anxiously. She could see no one.

"Did… did we shake him off?" she panted.

Errol was bent over next to her, also gasping for breath. He shook his head. "No," he said. "No… I don't think he even tried to run after us."

"But why not?" asked Wilson, taken aback.

"How would I know?" said Errol. He straightened up and looked at Ava, who was still looking nervously around. "I'm sorry about everything," he said.

He took off his jacket and held it out to her. Ava took it and hung it over her shoulders.

"Let's get you home, Ava," said Errol. "Your mums are worried sick about you."

Errol and Ava started walking, but Wilson lingered for just a second longer.

A sense of foreboding was nagging at her.

She was sure they hadn't seen the last of Leo Faber.

18

Front-page news

That night Wilson slept badly. She woke with a start several times, her heart beating wildly in her throat, convinced she'd heard someone outside the Doll's House. Every time she dozed off, she had horrible muddled dreams full of flapping, frightened birds and golden cages.

It seemed she'd hardly closed her eyes when there was a soft knock on her door.

"Yes?" she croaked with a mouth that felt as if it had been stuffed with cotton wool.

The door opened and Gabriel peered into the room.

"Wha-a-a-at?" groaned Wilson and pulled the pillow over her head.

Gabriel cleared his throat. "Erm, I'm afraid I have bad news."

Wilson peeped out from under the pillow. Gabriel was holding a newspaper. Her stomach lurched. If it was in the paper, it had to be *really* bad news. Wilson sat up and took the paper from him. She immediately understood why Gabriel looked so upset. She didn't even have to look for the bad news. It was on the front page.

LESEEBA

WEEKLY NEWSPAPER

THE POSTBOX

{FREE}

EDITION: 792

HERE SHE IS! REWARD OFFERED FOR "BIRD GIRL"

In a surprising twist yesterday, *The Postbox* received a picture of the "bird girl" who had been spotted near Leseeba over the past few weeks.

Until now, Captain Chester Calitz, head of the local police, has dismissed rumours that a mysterious girl with wings is living somewhere in the vicinity as "utter rubbish". However, in the picture you can clearly see the figure of a girl with two large wings stretched out behind her.

Mr Leo Faber, owner of the Fun Land funfair currently in town, made this photo available to the media. He said he suspected that the girl was the daughter of a trapeze artist who had worked in his circus years ago. "I used to own the well-known Faber's Circus, which unfortunately had to close its tent flaps. The bird girl was kidnapped from the circus when she was a newborn baby," Faber told our editorial staff. "We would like to reunite her with her family."

He offered a reward to anyone who can provide more information about the bird girl.

Stunned, she lowered the newspaper.

"It's in other newspapers too," said Gabriel. "I looked on the internet. And it's all over social media as well. Sorry, Wilson."

Wilson sighed. "It's not your fault, Gabriel."

He sat down on her bed and put his hand on her shoulder. "Are you okay?"

But before Wilson could answer, she heard her mum calling. Her voice sounded shrill and anxious. "Gabriel! There are… there are people here! And they're taking photos!"

Gabriel and Wilson stared at each other wide-eyed. There were voices coming from outside the Doll's House.

Wilson gulped. She was beginning to understand Leo Faber's plan. By now he must have figured out where Rita and Zelna lived. Everyone in town knew the two bee farmers. If he had wanted to catch and kidnap Ava again, he could have done so by now. But he was clever. He was going to leave it to the media to find Ava. And then it would look as if *he* was the hero, the long-lost dad who had come to rescue her.

Gabriel stood up and went to the door. The moment he opened it, a chorus of voices rang out. Cameras were flashing and people were shouting questions.

"Where's the bird girl?"

"Have you seen her?"

"We heard that she's friends with the girl who lives here! Is that true?"

Wilson looked over Gabriel's shoulder. At least ten reporters had gathered in front of the Doll's House. Captain Calitz was standing to one side, watching with an unhappy frown.

"Sorry, no comment!" shouted Gabriel and closed the door in their faces.

Wilson's mum was pacing around, flustered. She was already in her tennis gear, and on her shoulder was the sports bag with her two rackets sticking out the top. "What about my tennis camp?" she asked. "I have to be there in half an hour."

Wilson could hardly believe her ears. How on earth could her mum be thinking about *tennis* when they had reporters gathered outside their front door like a flock of vultures?

Tap-tap-tap.

"I said, no comment!" called Gabriel.

But Wilson frowned. She was quite sure the knocking wasn't coming from the front door. It sounded as though it was in her bedroom. She stepped back and pulled the curtains open.

A nose was pressed flat against the window, two jug ears peeping out from under a blue beanie.

"Errol!" she said.

Errol gestured for her to open the window.

Wilson lifted the latch. The window wasn't very big, but Errol hoisted himself up and wriggled through the opening. He landed on her bed like a sack of potatoes. Wilson folded her arms self-consciously. She'd forgotten she was still in her pyjamas. But Errol didn't seem to notice.

"Have you seen the newspaper?" he asked.

Wilson nodded as she pulled a jumper over her head.

"The town is full of reporters," he said. "They were at my gran's house as well. Granny Betty chased them off the front porch with her dressmaking scissors."

"Well, I probably don't have to tell you whose fault this is," said Wilson. "By now Ava's photo is all over the world."

Errol looked ashamed. "Yes, okay," he mumbled. "I *said* I was sorry, didn't I?"

"Wilson, who're you talking to?" called Gabriel.

"It's Errol!" she replied.

Errol jumped up from the bed. "We have to make a plan," he said. "Before all those reporters get hold of Ava."

Wilson bit her lower lip. "Maybe Zelna and Rita have already made a plan," she said. "Maybe they've fled with Ava."

The two mums had been very relieved to see Ava the day before – but also very upset when they heard what had happened. Worst of all, they couldn't ask the police for help. They had raised Ava for all those years without legally adopting her, and they had kept her existence a secret. Gabriel said you could end up in jail for something like that.

Wilson's mum came into the room, the sports bag still over her shoulder.

"How am I going to plough through all those reporters? This town is getting too much for me. I think it's time we leave."

Wilson tilted her head. The two rackets sticking out above her mum's shoulders looked familiar somehow.

Strangely, Wilson thought back to something her mum had said earlier.

"This whole story sounds to me like a prank or a... scam. A girl with wings... that just cannot exist."

Slowly but surely a plan was taking shape in Wilson's head.

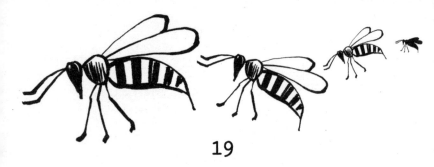

19

A swarm of wasps

Wilson might have thought of the plan first, but she had to admit that Gabriel helped with the finer details. All the years that he'd worked at a newspaper proved to be useful.

When their plan was ready, Gabriel opened the door of the Doll's House. The group of reporters started buzzing like a swarm of wasps.

Gabriel cleared his throat and raised his hand for silence. "We've decided to tell you the truth about the bird girl," he announced. "It's high time the world is informed. An official press conference will be held this afternoon."

"Where?" called a voice.

"What time?" someone else wanted to know.

Gabriel hesitated. Wilson buried her head in her hands. Okay, maybe they should have discussed it in more detail.

"Erm… four o'clock this afternoon," said Gabriel. "Right here in the caravan park."

"No!" hissed Wilson's mum. "Do you want this lot here at our door *again*?"

"Erm... I mean... erm... in the small park opposite the town library," said Gabriel. "You are all welcome. Until then, we are not going to answer any further questions. So, can we please make breakfast in peace and quiet now? There are some vegan sausages in the fridge with my name on them."

A snigger rippled through the group of reporters. They seemed to be satisfied with this arrangement. One by one, they left.

Captain Calitz had been watching the scene with an annoyed frown. When the last reporter had left,

he shot Wilson and the others an irritated look.

"Peace and quiet!" he grumbled. "That's asking a lot. I don't know what you all are up to, but I don't like it. Newspapers! Media conferences! Reporters all over town! Rubbish about a so-called bird girl! No, I don't like this one bit. Hmph."

He got on his bicycle and pedalled off with a straight back.

"Thank goodness!" sighed Wilson's mum. "I wish I could stay to help with your plan, but my tennis children are waiting. Will you be okay?"

"As long as we can borrow two of your old rackets," said Wilson.

Her mum nodded. She seemed relieved that she could flee from all the strange things that had been happening lately at the Doll's House.

"I'll be keeping my fingers crossed that your plan works!" she called over her shoulder as she rushed off to the tennis court.

Wilson looked at Errol. She was trying very hard not to think of all the ways their plan could go wrong. "I hope your gran will be able to help us," she said.

Errol nodded. "My gran can make magic."

20
Granny Betty

"Ah, Wilson!" said Granny Betty when she opened the door. "How lovely to see you again. I suppose this is your dad?"

"Gabriel," said Gabriel and shook her hand.

"Stepdad," muttered Wilson.

"Pleased to meet you, Gabriel," said Granny Betty. "Errol should have brought you over long ago – after all, you live just across the road. We're practically neighbours. Come inside, come inside."

"Erm… we need your help," said Wilson, coming straight to the point.

"Help?" asked Granny Betty. "Any time. But let me make us some tea first, and then you can tell me how I can help."

Wilson had never known her two grandmothers, but Granny Betty's house looked exactly how she imagined a grandmother's house would look. The wooden floors smelled of polish, there was lovely old furniture with curly feet and flowery patterns, the curtains were heavy and thick, and a large ginger cat was sleeping in a sunny patch on the windowsill.

After making sure that everyone had tea and biscuits, Granny Betty sat down with a soft groan on one of the couches in the lounge.

"So, how can I help you?" she asked.

Wilson, Gabriel and Errol looked at each other.

They hadn't decided who would do the talking.

Wilson elbowed Errol. She was *his* grandma, so *he* should ask.

"Erm… Granny Betty, I'm in a bit of trouble…" he muttered.

Granny Betty lowered her cup with the floral pattern and peered over her glasses frowning worriedly. "Trouble, Errol dear?" she asked. "What kind of trouble?"

Looking embarrassed, Errol scratched behind one of his jug ears. "Well… the kind of trouble you'd rather not tell anyone about," he said.

Granny Betty sighed and took a sip of tea. "Just how bad is the trouble you are in?" she asked. "And what do you need to do to get out of it?"

"It's not only *Errol dear* who's in trouble," Wilson came to the rescue.

Errol shot her a side look.

"Actually, it's all three of us who are in trouble," Wilson continued. "So, erm… all three of us came to ask for your help."

"It's the kind of trouble that you can fix with a needle and thread, Gran," said Errol.

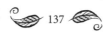

Granny Betty shook her head and giggled. "All right then – at least that sounds like the best kind of trouble. Tell me what I can do."

Wilson took the two tennis rackets out of her backpack. As she and Errol took turns to explain what they wanted, Granny Betty started to look worried. But when they were done, she nodded.

"I suppose I shouldn't ask *why* you need this," she said. "But I'm sure I can make it."

Errol flashed a proud I-told-you smile at Wilson and Gabriel.

"Before half past three, please, Gran," he said.

21

The press conference

A few minutes before four o'clock the small park opposite the town library was a hive of activity. There were many more people than the handful of reporters that had gathered outside the Doll's House that morning. It seemed to Wilson like the entire town had shown up to attend the press conference. Even Miss Hannah, the librarian, could not contain her curiosity. She was standing there, sucking in her cheeks, and glowering at everyone as if she was about to scold them for making so much noise.

Captain Calitz was also there. He hovered around in the background with his moustache twitching even more than usual. He didn't seem to know what he was supposed to be doing.

Gabriel dug out a handkerchief from his trouser pocket and wiped the beads of sweat from his forehead. He looked like an actor who was about to go on stage but couldn't remember his lines.

"Relax," said Wilson. "Everything will be okay."

She wasn't sure who she was trying to calm down – Gabriel or herself.

"Are you sure about this?" her mum whispered. But the confused look on her face made it clear that she didn't really understand what was going on. She'd been coaching tennis all day, so she hadn't been part of the planning.

"This is the only way we can help Ava," Wilson told her mum.

Gabriel pointed at his watch. It was four o'clock on the dot.

In the centre of the small park was a huge old oak.

Wilson and Gabriel walked to the tree. Wilson had to force herself not to look up.

Gabriel positioned himself in the shade of the tree and cleared his throat. Silence descended on the assembled crowd. Wilson gave him a thumbs-up.

"Good afternoon," said Gabriel.

"Thank you all for coming. As I promised you this morning, we are here to tell the truth about Leseeba's... erm... bird girl."

Excited whispers rippled through the crowd.

"By now all of you have probably seen the photo in the paper and online," Gabriel continued. "The whole world is buzzing about the girl with wings. Well, *I* was the photographer who took that photo."

There was a series of audible gasps and reporters immediately started firing questions.

Gabriel raised his hand.

"Please let me finish," he said. "That photograph wasn't meant to drive everyone into a frenzy. I'm sorry about that."

"Where is she?" called a voice from the crowd. "Where is the bird girl?"

A slight smile crept across Gabriel's face. He looked up into the tree. The group of people followed his lead.

Wilson held her breath.

Then came the first shocked scream.

"It's her! The bird girl!"

Chaos broke out. People were gesturing and talking excitedly, cameras were flashing, and reporters were elbowing each other out of the way to get as close as possible to the tree.

"Wait!" called Gabriel. "I'm not done yet!"

Slowly the group calmed down.

Gabriel pointed at the figure sitting on a branch above his head. "Meet the bird girl," he said.

The figure slowly stood upright on the branch and waved at the crowd. Everyone was staring dumbfounded at the two wings protruding behind the slender shoulders of the bird girl. Brown feathers shimmered in the afternoon sun.

A sharp voice suddenly pierced the stunned silence. "That's no girl! That's Errol Abrahams. I'd recognise those jug ears anywhere!"

A sea of faces turned to Miss Hannah. The librarian was pointing a threatening finger at Errol.

"You still owe me a library book!" she called out. "Don't think I've forgotten about that."

The quiet murmurs grew into a chaotic din.

The crowd was laughing and pointing at the figure on the branch.

Wilson stuck her fingers in her ears.

"Silence!" shouted Gabriel. "Silence, please! Give me a chance to finish."

It took a while before the crowd settled down again.

"This whole thing was supposed to be an innocent prank," explained Gabriel. "Errol's grandmother made him a pair of wings – by the way, she's a brilliant seamstress, as you can see, so do go to her if you want to have clothes made or adjusted."

One of the reporters, a woman with blonde hair tied

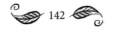

up in a tight bun, raised her hand. "Am I getting this right?" she asked. "Is that a boy up there in the tree?"

Before Gabriel even had a chance to reply, Errol pulled the black wig off his head. "This thing makes me itch," he grumbled.

A couple of people snorted with laughter.

"Errol, why did you try to trick the whole town?" another reporter called out.

Errol looked at Gabriel and Wilson inquiringly. He didn't seem to know how to reply.

Wilson nodded at him, encouragingly.

"Erm… it was just a silly prank," he said. "I didn't really think the newspaper would believe me when I told them about the bird girl. But when the story ended up in the paper, I decided to ask my gran to make me wings… I wanted to see if people were dumb enough to fall for it."

The group of reporters muttered among themselves. A few locals shook their heads and walked off, grumbling. They didn't want anyone to think they'd actually fallen for the story of the bird girl.

"Wait!" a loud voice called unexpectedly.

A tall man came marching through the crowd. He was in such a hurry that he was shoving people out of the way. When he reached the front, he turned to the sea of faces.

"It's all hogwash!" he roared. "The bird girl *does* exist! Her name is Ava."

Wilson gasped and shot Gabriel and Errol an anxious look. Oh no, this wasn't part of the plan…

"Who are you?" called a reporter.

"My name is Leo Faber," said the man with the bushy mane of hair. He had such a booming voice that it was easy to believe he'd once been a ringmaster. "I'm the owner of the funfair that's in town now. Ava is my daughter. One of these days you'll be able to come to my funfair and look at the bird girl – the *real* bird girl, one with *real* wings!"

The funfair owner looked surprised when everyone burst out laughing. No one seemed to be listening to him – everyone's eyes were fixed on the tree. Wilson couldn't resist laughing herself. Errol was trying to balance on one leg on the branch. He was making comical movements with his arms, as if trying to fly.

"Stop that!" roared Leo Faber. "Can't you see that little cheat isn't the real bird girl? I paid him to… to—"

"He paid Errol to make everyone believe the bird girl really exists!" Wilson called out.

Faber blinked and slowly turned to her.

Wilson gulped.

"Then he wanted Errol to act like he was her, so that everyone would pay to come and see him," she continued. Words were gushing out of her mouth without her even having to think what to say next.

"It's a lie!" yelled the owner of the funfair. "Don't believe a word she's saying!"

But most of the people had already turned to leave. The photographers were packing away their cameras.

"I can't believe I wasted my time on this," said the reporter with the blonde bun as she stuffed her pen and notebook into her handbag. "I drove all the way to this dusty little town for nothing."

There was at least one face in the crowd that looked pleased. Captain Calitz. Under his moustache something appeared that Wilson had never seen there before – a smile.

22

Four million flowers

LESEEBA

WEEKLY NEWSPAPER | **THE POSTBOX** | {FREE}

EDITION: 793

"BIRD GIRL" A CHILDISH PRANK

Owner of funfair wanted to capitalise on innocent stunt

The so-called "bird girl" who had lately been spotted near Leseeba and who has had the locals in a flutter, has turned out to be a boy with a pair of home-made wings of feathers, fabric and two old tennis rackets. The prank that Errol Abrahams (12) played on everyone caused a media uproar and had the internet buzzing after a picture of the "bird girl" had gone viral.

Wilson read the article twice before looking up. She smiled at Gabriel. "Thank you," she said. "You were incredible."

Gabriel nodded. He looked quite pleased with himself.

"The two of you make a good team," said Wilson's mum, smiling.

Wilson rolled her eyes. She sincerely hoped her mum wasn't thinking that she and Gabriel would soon be going on dad-and-daughter outings to drink pink milkshakes and fly kites in the park. As a matter of principle, Wilson *never* ordered a pink milkshake anyway. It reminded her too much of princesses and ponies and pyjama parties.

"It's true. You were brilliant, Wilson," said Errol. "That story you plucked out of nowhere about Faber paying me to dress up like a bird girl was brilliant."

"Thanks, Errol dear," said Wilson. "I must say, you make a really cute girl."

"Hmph," muttered Errol, managing to sound exactly like a certain policeman.

It was a lovely sunny Friday morning. The four were sitting on camping chairs in front of the Doll's House. For breakfast, Gabriel had cooked delicious vegan burgers on the barbecue.

Wilson looked up when she heard a vehicle approaching.

A green pickup truck appeared and pulled up near them.

Wilson smiled when she saw Ava's mums climb out.

"Rita and Zelna!" She jumped up and ran to greet them.

The two women hugged her and made their way over to the others.

"Meet Ava's two mums," Wilson formally introduced the adults to each other for the first time "They have a bee farm, but Rita used to be a horse whisperer in the circus, and Zelna a fire breather."

Wilson's mum looked astonished. She had never met a horse whisperer and a fire breather in real life.

But Zelna was staring at Wilson's mum in equal astonishment.

"My goodness!" she exclaimed. "Aren't you Donna Taylor? You were my hero! Back in the day, I never missed a single match you played in!"

Wilson's mum turned as red as a tomato.

"We brought you something from the farm," said Ma Rita. "Just something small." She handed Wilson a jar of honey.

"Thanks a lot," said Wilson. "But this isn't something small at all. Honeybees have to visit four million flowers to make one kilogram of honey."

The two mums laughed.

"I can tell who you've been spending time with!" said Zelna.

For a while, the adults chatted about tennis ("Wimbledon ticket prices aren't what they used to be"), newspaper reporters ("Newspapers aren't what they used to be either") and the weather ("It isn't as cold as other years – these days winters aren't what they used to be"). Wilson and Errol stood about, bored.

When the adults finally ran out of things to say, Zelna and Rita turned to the two children.

"We want to thank you both from the bottom of our hearts," said Zelna. "Not only because you saved Ava from the clutches of that evil Faber – but also because you came up with such a smart plan."

"The funfair has left," said Rita. "They started taking down everything yesterday afternoon, and this morning there was no sign of the rides and stalls."

Wilson gulped. "And Ava?" she asked. "How is she doing?"

The two mums looked at each other. It seemed they didn't quite know what to say.

"She misses the two of you," said Zelna. "She says hi."

"This whole thing upset her terribly," said Rita.

Wilson summoned up her courage and asked one of the questions that had kept her awake the previous night. "Is Leo Faber really her dad?"

Zelna smiled wryly. "No, Wilson. Faber isn't Ava's dad. I can assure you of that."

"The night before Ava was born, her mum told us about Ava's dad." Rita's voice and eyes were soft. "She said he'd come from another country, a faraway warm country where the trees are green all year and the birds sing differently from those here. She said he'd gone back there, and never knew a baby was on the way."

The sadness in Rita's voice caught Wilson unaware and she had to blink hard to fight back her tears.

"We're worried," said Zelna with a sigh. "Faber knows where Ava is. The funfair may have left, but I know him, and he's not going to give up that easily. He hasn't been looking for Ava for years for nothing."

"So, what are you going to do?" asked Wilson.

The two women looked at each other.

"We don't really have a choice, said Zelna. "We'll have to up and leave, find somewhere else to live."

A stunned silence descended on the small group. Wilson could only imagine how tough it would be for the two women to pack up and leave, the same way they'd had to leave the circus years ago.

Errol had been quiet all this time, so Wilson was surprised when he cleared his throat.

"I have something for you," he said. "Please give this to Ava."

He unzipped his jacket and took out a brown envelope from his inside pocket. He handed it to Zelna. She opened it and took out three photos.

Wilson suddenly wished she had smiled at the camera that day, so that Ava could remember her like that.

"I only gave Faber one photo," said Errol. "Luckily, it was the one where you can't see her face that clearly. And luckily that wasn't the one with Wilson and me next to her – otherwise no one would've believed our story."

"Thanks a lot, Errol," said Rita.

"May we see her?" asked Wilson. "One last time? To say goodbye?"

23
We are not alone

It was late afternoon. The sun was setting and could almost touch the treetops. In an hour or two it would be dark. Somewhere among the reeds, an Egyptian goose was calling sorrowfully.

Wilson and Errol were sitting on their usual patch of grass next to the lake. They took it in turns to throw pebbles into the water.

"Wilson, can I ask you something?" Errol wanted to know.

Wilson tossed another pebble in the water.

Plop!

"Since when do you ask permission to ask questions?" she muttered, checking her watch.

"I saw your name on those rackets that Granny Betty used to make the wings. Were you named after a racket?"

Wilson grinned. "Yep. As you've probably realised, my mum is quite serious about tennis."

"Okay," said Errol. "That's cool."

There was a rustling behind them. Wilson turned around and smiled.

Ava appeared from among the trees. She was wearing a padded jacket. If you didn't know what she was hiding inside it, you would just think it was too big for her.

"Hi Ava!" said Wilson and Errol.

Ava walked up to them and, without a word, pulled them both into a tight embrace. She didn't *need* to say anything – Wilson knew exactly what this meant.

"It's not easy to be the only one of your kind, is it?" said Wilson. She could feel the soft feathers on Ava's neck.

Ava shook her head.

"Wilson is also one of a kind," said Errol. "She's the only person on earth who's been named after a tennis racket."

They burst out laughing, and Wilson quickly wiped away the tears that had unexpectedly sprung from her eyes.

"I want to show you guys something," said Ava. "But you have to keep it a secret."

"Of course," said Errol. "We're *very* good at keeping secrets."

Wilson and Ava both looked at him with raised eyebrows.

"What?" he asked indignantly.

Ava took a folded piece of paper from her jacket pocket. She opened it and held it out to Wilson and Errol. Wilson looked at it curiously.

It was a printout of an email someone had sent to Zelna, someone with a very strange name. In the subject line it read: *You are not alone.*

Attached to the email were photos.

Five photos.

There was a boy with curly blond hair.

A girl with short dark hair.

A toddler holding a doll.

Twin boys with identical pixie noses and a naughty glint in their eyes.

And an older boy with a frown on his face, who looked like he could be in high school.

All six children had wings.

Wilson's mouth dropped open. "Does this mean…?"

Ava shrugged. "I'm not sure exactly what it means. But maybe it means… I'm not completely alone."

"Erm… you guys, we aren't alone either," said Errol. The strange unsteadiness in his voice made Wilson look up sharply.

Her stomach tightened.

How long had the man been standing there, watching them?

When the children turned to look at him in horror, a smile appeared on Leo Faber's face. Slowly he walked up to them. The late-afternoon sun made his hair glow as if it were on fire.

"Hello Ava," he said calmly. "I have come to fetch you."

Ava took a step back. "No," she said. "Leave me alone. I don't want anything to do with you."

"The funfair is moving on to the next town," said Faber, as if he hadn't heard what she'd said. "And you're coming with me. That's where you belong. Those two women can't give you the life you deserve hidden away in this dusty little town."

"It's *my* life," said Ava firmly. "Ma Zelna and Ma Rita are good to me."

Faber sighed and shook his head, as if listening to a particularly boring song on the radio. "Your mum destroyed my circus," he growled, and for the first time there was a dark edge to his voice. "She was my star attraction, and when she ran away, the circus struggled. Then she reappeared out of the blue, only to leave us again for good. But do you know why she came back, little Ava? She wanted to say she was sorry for letting us, her circus family, down. That's why she brought us a gift. A gift that could save the circus. *You*, little Ava, were her special gift. And if those two good-for-nothing women hadn't stolen you, the circus would never have gone under."

Wilson had heard enough.

"He's mad," she said. "Ava, you have to run! Run!"

Something flashed in Faber's hand.

Wilson shuddered.

A knife.

Ava saw it too.

She took another step back and took off her jacket and hat.

Faber froze, his eyes wide with anticipation.

Fwwwp-fwwwp.

Faber drew in his breath sharply, mesmerised by Ava's wings. "My birdie," he said. "Your wings… They're even more spectacular here than in the cramped caravan. See, you can't hide those from the world!"

Fwwwp-fwwwp.

Ava wheeled around and started to run.

"Come back!" roared Faber and chased after her.

Ava headed straight for the nearest big tree. Wilson's heart was pounding as the bird girl flapped her way up the thick tree trunk. For a moment, she

vanished among the dense leaves, and then Wilson
spotted her high up on a branch.

But she didn't stay there.

Fwwwp-fwwwp.

Gobsmacked, Wilson watched as Ava leapt forward,
spread her wings... and glided to the next tree. Faber
was stomping around like a hungry predator frustrated
that its prey was escaping.

Fwwwp-fwwwp.

Ava swooped to the next tree.

"Good for you, Ava!" Errol cheered. "Fly away!"

Watching the girl glide gracefully from one tree to
the next, Wilson was so transfixed that she didn't notice
what Faber was doing. As quick as a flash, he grabbed
her with one arm and, with the other, he held the knife
against her throat.

"No!"

Her scream echoed among the trees.

Then everything went quiet. Faber's face was so
close to hers that Wilson could smell his breath.
Clearly, he wasn't good friends with his toothbrush.

"Ava!" Faber shouted. "Come back, my birdie, or
your friends are going to get hurt."

Silence. Even the trees seemed to be holding their
breath.

"Ava... don't... listen... to him!" Wilson struggled
to force the words out.

Out of the corner of her eye, Wilson caught a sudden movement. Errol was diving through the air with a log in his hands. "Let go of her!" he screamed and swung the log at Faber.

Faber laughed a wicked laugh, as he caught the log and hurled it back in Errol's direction, propelling him to the ground. Errol gasped for breath.

"Ava?" called Faber. "I know you can hear me. Look what has happened… Poor Errol's hurt and it's your fault. You don't want the girlie to get hurt as well, do you? If you come with me, I'll set your friends free."

Somewhere in her befuddled brain Wilson managed for a moment to wonder what was up with funfair people and the word *girlie*.

Fwwwp-fwwwp.

Wilson looked up.

Ava landed on the ground beside them.

"No," muttered Wilson. "Ava…"

Faber released her and shoved her roughly aside. She tripped and tumbled onto the grass next to Errol.

When she looked up, Faber was already beside Ava. He grabbed her. Her head and her wings were hanging limply. She didn't even try to pull free.

"Come on, let's go. My van is not far. By tonight we'll be—"

"Let go of her!" thundered a voice.

Wilson looked around.

Captain Calitz slammed on the brakes and jumped off his bicycle. He was surprisingly agile for a man of his age.

"I said, let go of the girl!" he ordered, dangling a pair of metal handcuffs.

Faber lifted Ava up as if she was a feather and held her in front of his chest. "If you come after me, the bird girls gets it," he said.

Captain Calitz hesitated. Wilson's mouth was bone dry.

Faber started walking backwards with Ava still pressed tightly to his chest, like a shield between him and the policeman.

Wilson felt as if time stood still.

Several thoughts flashed through her mind.

Her dad living overseas with his ordinary family in his ordinary house, and how she planned to visit one day when things had calmed down.

Her mum's tennis lessons.

Gabriel with his camera and his photos of dogs wearing bow ties.

The Doll's House.

Errol with his jug ears and his unusually broad smile that was as infectious as chicken pox.

Zelna and Rita, the bee farmers who used to work in a circus.

And, of course, Ava. The bird girl.

Wilson slowly breathed out and focused. She tilted her head to the side. The log Errol that had hurled Errol to the ground was lying right next to her.

Faber wasn't paying her any attention. His eyes were glued to the policeman.

Wilson quietly crouched down and picked up the log.

Then she catapulted herself through the air.

She swung the log as hard as she could.

Dwang!

The log hit the back of Faber's head with a muffled whack.

He released Ava from his grasp and toppled over with a grunt.

Wilson stared at Faber, lying motionless at her feet. Her legs were shaking and her arms ached.

Errol sat up with a groan.

"Superhero," he said.

For a moment, Wilson had no idea what he was talking about. But then she grinned. "Snail slime."

Wilson hurried over to Ava. She wrapped her arms around the bird girl's shoulders. Ava's wings were quivering. "It's okay," Wilson said. "He can't hurt you any more."

Captain Calitz crouched over Faber and clicked the handcuffs around his wrists. "I'm going to make sure he spends a long, long time in jail," he said. "Attempted kidnapping of two children. That's a serious charge."

Wilson frowned. "*Two* children?" she asked.

Captain Calitz nodded. "You two can be glad that you escaped his clutches."

To Wilson's surprise, he looked only at her and Errol.

Not once did he look at Ava. Not even for a millisecond.

"But what about—"

"Leseeba is a lovely place to live," Captain Calitz continued. "A peaceful town where everyone knows each other. The perfect place to retire. And that's exactly what I'm going to do in a few months. I'm going to sit on my porch and drink tea and tend to my roses and enjoy the peace and quiet. I haven't been working to keep our town this peaceful all these years for nothing!"

Wilson glanced over at Ava. "And what about her?" she asked.

Captain Calitz shrugged. "Who? Who are you talking about? All I see is a villain who has just tried to kidnap two children. You two had better get home now. I'll come by later to speak to your families and take statements."

A smile slowly spread over Wilson's face.

Captain Calitz was deliberately pretending not to have seen Ava. He was going to keep her existence a secret as long as he could retire in peace and quiet and tend to his prize-winning roses.

Maybe Zelna and Rita didn't have to sell the bee farm and move away after all.

That sounded like a brilliant plan to Wilson.

24
You're weird, Wilson Taylor

It was almost dark by the time Captain Calitz had taken statements from Wilson and Errol. They had all met up at Granny Betty's house. Errol's grandma had served tea and biscuits while the policeman spoke to everyone. The adults were, of course, horrified by what they heard.

"Faber probably wanted revenge because the newspapers had found out that his story about the so-called bird girl was a lie," said Captain Calitz and shook his head disapprovingly. "That man is dangerous. He'll be put behind bars for a long time. I hope this was the last time that—"

"But Ava does really exist!" Wilson's mum interrupted him.

"I hope this is the last time that a funfair comes to Leseeba," continued Captain Calitz, finishing his sentence as if Wilson's mum had not just spoken.

Wilson and Errol stood on the pavement and watched the police captain hop on his bicycle and pedal off.

"Now all he has to do is solve the mystery of the garden-gnome thief," said Wilson, "and then he can finally retire in peace."

"I sometimes wonder if there's more than one of him," said Errol. "Do you think Captain Calitz has been cloned? You know, maybe there are a dozen Captain Calitzes riding around on bikes in our town. How else does he always manage to show up out of the blue, no matter where there's trouble?"

Wilson just smiled. If there was one thing she'd learnt over the last few days, it was not to reply to Errol's do-you-think questions.

Wilson's mum and Gabriel waved goodnight to Granny Betty and started walking back to the caravan park together. Wilson stayed in the street with Errol for a while longer.

The last rays of sun were glowing on the roof of the Doll's House, painting the clouds and treetops pink.

"I think sunset clouds taste like candyfloss," said Wilson.

Errol nodded. "You're weird, Wilson Taylor."

"Yep," said Wilson. "I wasn't named after a tennis racket for nothing."

As she walked away, she could hear Errol roaring with laughter. She couldn't help smiling too.

Back at the Doll's House, Gabriel cooked dinner on the barbecue – stuffed mushrooms and kebabs made of sweet potato, beetroot and butternut squash. While they ate, Gabriel told them what he had photographed that day – a spider's web, an axe and an old-fashioned coffee jar. Wilson's mum told them about a boy in her tennis class whose mouth was so big that he could fit an entire a tennis ball in it, like a dog. This story had Wilson and Gabriel crying with laughter.

When it was bedtime, Wilson's mum sat down next to her on the bed.

"Are you okay?" she asked and stroked her hair, the way she had used to do when Wilson was little.

Wilson nodded.

"If you want to talk about what happened, remember that Gabriel and I will always be here for you."

"I know. Thanks."

Her mum kissed her on the forehead. "Sleep tight."

Long after her mum had switched off the light, Wilson was still lying awake. She heard her mum and Gabriel lock the front door of the Doll's House, brush their teeth, say goodnight to each other and grow quiet. She lay there, listening to a dog barking somewhere in the distance, and after a while she could hear Gabriel snoring lightly.

Wilson knew that before long her mum and Gabriel would decide to pack up everything, hit the road and move on to the next town. She was going to miss Errol and Ava and Zelna and Rita, and this wonderful adventure she'd had in Leseeba. Hopefully the next town would have a friendlier librarian. No matter how hard she tried, Wilson could not imagine that she would miss Miss Hannah.

But over the past few days she had slowly but surely realised something.

The world is an extraordinary place, full of secrets and adventures.

It was fun to be a part of it.

And what better way to experience all of this than to roam around in a teeny-tiny house on wheels with two peculiar characters like her mum and Gabriel?

She didn't need to wait for the day when an ordinary family who lived in an ordinary house would decide the time was right for her to become part of their ordinary life.

You're weird, Wilson Taylor.

Errol was right. Had she not been a teensy-weensy bit weird, she would never have been able to be friends with Errol and Ava, and the past few days would never have happened.

Wilson pushed her duvet aside, got up and turned the light back on. She opened her wardrobe door.

For a while she stared at the advert.

Then she took it down, scrunched it up into a ball and tossed it in the bin.

With a smile she climbed back into bed.

As she was falling asleep, Wilson was sure she could hear the rustling of wings somewhere outside in the dark night.

Jaco Jacobs is the most popular and prolific children's book author in Afrikaans. He has written many books including *A Good Day for Climbing Trees* and *A Good Night for Shooting Zombies* and has sold over a million copies worldwide. Jaco's work has been translated into English, Dutch, Italian, Slovenian and Spanish. He lives in Bloemfontein, South Africa.

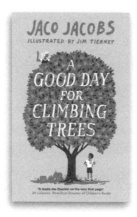

A GOOD NIGHT FOR SHOOTING ZOMBIES

Translated by Kobus Geldenhuys

Illustrations by Jim Tierney

'A wonderful and exciting story with true emotional depth.'

Ross Welford, author of *Time Travelling with a Hamster*

SOMETIMES THE END IS JUST THE BEGINNING
OF A NEW ADVENTURE

Martin likes perfect numbers. He also likes to stick
to his own perfect daily routine.

But one day, Martin meets his neighbour, a boy called Vusi.
Vusi dreams of making a zombie movie but he's not got much time.
Before they know it, the two are plunged into a wild adventure,
pulling everyone they know along with them.

Stay up to date with all the news from Rock the Boat
@RockTheBoatNews and rocktheboatbooks.com